Granny

Constance Horne

Constance Horne

Cover and illustrations by
Don Bescoe

gage EDUCATIONAL PUBLISHING COMPANY
A DIVISION OF CANADA PUBLISHING CORPORATION
TORONTO ONTARIO CANADA

Canadian Cataloguing in Publication Data
Horne, Constance E.
Nykola and Granny

(Jeanpac paperback original)
ISBN 0-7715-7019-8

I. Bescoe, Don. II. Title. III. Series:
Jean pac paperback original.

PS8565.076N94 1988 jC813'.54 C88-094156-1
PZ.H663Ny 1988

Design: Marc Mireault

ISBN: 0-7715-**7019-8**

2 3 4 5 6 7 8 9 WC 96 95 94 93 92

Written, Printed, and Bound in Canada

CONTENTS

CHAPTER 1

Left Behind

One hot, Sunday afternoon, in the summer of 1899, Nykola Ganczer[1] walked slowly down the narrow road to the edge of the little village in the Ukraine where he lived with his uncle, Feodor Urbanovitch[2]. Sundays were always sad days for him. It was then that he most missed his family.

It was three months ago now that his father, mother, and two sisters had gone off to the new world and left him behind.

Granny often comforted him. "Oh, my Nykolenko, little pigeon," she murmured, "you know they did not want to leave you. You were so sick with the fever! What else could they do?"

Uncle Feodor would only scold Nykola for moping about being left behind. "Did you expect your father to wait for a sick child?" he demanded.

[1]Ni'ku lə Gan'zer
[2]Fē'ə dôr Er ban ō'vich

"How could he? He had sold all he owned, including his land, and spent the money for steamship tickets. Did you think *I* would keep Wasyl[3] Ganczer and his family? Just because his wife is sister to mine? Bah! Bad enough he has left you to be a burden to me. Well, you're old enough to earn your keep, and earn it you will. There's plenty of work to be done in the fields."

Nykola sat down on the warm stones of the low wall that marked the boundary of one of his uncle's three fields. Across the road were other small fields owned by other peasants. Beyond them lay low hills covered with woods, the property of a rich Austrian lord. Nestled at the edge of the wood stood a small onion-domed church.

Nykola always thought of it as Granny's church. During his illness, she told him, she had gone there every day to pray for him. She had also nursed him carefully, so that he was now strong and well again. Much stronger than his cousin, Petro. What a weakling, with his pale face and skinny arms! Nykola's skin was brown from the sun, he had thick, dark hair, and large hands and feet. His father said this meant he would be a big man one day. His mother said that his

[3]Va'sil

dark eyes with their long lashes were just like his Uncle Stefan's[4] and some day he would be as handsome as that young man.

Oh, if only he could have gone to live with Uncle Stefan, his father's brother. But Stefan was too young to own his own fields. He worked on the estate of a rich Polish landowner and lived in a dormitory with the other farm hands. Just as Nykola was thinking about his uncle, a young man came into sight walking toward the village.

Could it be? Yes!

"It is Uncle Stefan!" he shouted. He jumped up and ran toward him.

[4]Ste fän′

Stefan, too, began to run, waving something over his head.

"A letter! From your father!" he called.

Nykola stopped abruptly. A letter? Word from his family at last? When Stefan reached him, he gazed at the paper with wide eyes.

"Is it for me?" he asked in a low voice.

"Well, it's addressed to me but, of course, it's for you, too. Come, let's find your Granny and the others and I'll read it out loud."

In a few minutes the whole family had gathered round the young man in the tiny front yard.

Wasyl Ganczer wrote that he and his wife had settled on a farm near the town of Dauphin in Manitoba. The foreign-sounding names made Nykola's cousins giggle.

"I think it is a fine name for a town!" said Nykola.

"The name of the town matters little," said Stefan impatiently. "Listen to the description of his farm. He says, 'I have one hundred and sixty acres of land for which I paid just ten dollars to the land agent. . .' "

"One hundred and sixty acres!" Feodor stared at Stefan for a moment and then slapped his thigh. "No! I don't believe it! What would a man do with so much land?"

"Nevertheless, he has it," Stefan insisted. He continued reading. "About two-thirds of the farm is woodland and we have..."

Anna gasped. "So much wood? And on their own land?"

Stefan spoke loudly and firmly. " '...we have built a small house from our own trees and will be sheltered for the winter.' " The family listened in wonder to the rest of the letter. Finally, Stefan looked up and smiled at Nykola. " 'How is my son, Nykola Ganczer?' " he read. " 'His mother and I grieve because he is not with us. When I can, I will send you money. Next spring will you bring him to us? I have taken a homestead in an area where there is plenty of vacant land so that you will be able to settle near us. Write to me about the health of my son and tell me when you will bring him to me. Marfa Slyzuk sends greetings to you, to her son, to her sister, Anna Slyzuk, and to her mother, Tetiana Doroshenko[5].' "

Everyone began talking at once after Stefan refolded the letter.

"So much land!"

[5]Te tē än'a Do ru shen'ko

"Canada! Manitoba! What funny names!"

"Dauphin! Dauphin!"

The children all burst into giggles and Feodor roared at them to run and play. Nykola stayed with the adults.

"So," said Feodor, "a man may get rich just by going to this new land! The agent told us so, but I, for one, didn't believe him. One hundred and sixty acres! No, it is impossible!"

"But," argued Stefan, tapping the letter with his palm, "he says he has it."

Feodor stood up. He stretched his arms, making his huge muscles bulge under the embroidered Sunday shirt. He grunted. "I would like to see this land," he said.

"Well, you should," exclaimed Stefan. He pushed a lock of black hair from his eyes. "Yes, you should! Why don't you go to the new land?"

"Why do I not go?" shouted Feodor. "Me? Why do I not go?" He waved his arms wildly. "Where would I get the money to buy steamship tickets for all my family? Eh? Can you tell me that? My wife and me, three girls, a sickly boy and a baby—that's seven souls. Do you know how much it would cost to take seven souls to this new land?" He shouted louder. "Could I borrow money? Ha! The moneylender would laugh at me. How would he get his money back from me? Do I know a rich landowner waiting to buy my fields like Wasyl had? Do I have sturdy sons to work for me in the new land? Bah!" He spat on the ground. "I have no money to go!"

"Well, I am going," declared Stefan.

"Go, go!" Feodor answered. "The more of you who go, the more land for the rest of us! Go!"

"I will, as soon as I can!"

"Will you take me, Uncle?" asked Nykola anxiously. Stefan winked at his nephew. "Of course, I will. I will take you to your father and mother."

"When?" cried Nykola.

"We must wait to hear from your father again." Stefan looked sad. "I have no money of my own. He will write again."

CHAPTER 2

No Passport

The second letter, which arrived in April, caused as much excitement as the first. Along with it came enough money for two people to travel to Manitoba. The Ukrainian peasants rarely used money, except for a few kopeks to spend in a tavern or to buy a trinket from a peddler. Before he brought this letter to Nykola, Stefan had changed the cheque into gold coins. On the Sunday he came, he called the whole family to gather round the table. After he read the letter, he reached inside his blouse, pulled out a coarse, canvas bag and, grinning broadly, spilled a shower of gold florins onto the table.

Anna gasped and all the children stared wide-eyed. Nykola felt as though he would burst with pride. All this money belonged to his father! He looked at Petro triumphantly. No longer would his cousin be able to taunt him about being dependent on Uncle Feodor. Now Nykola could escape from them all!

Petro reached out as if to touch one of the shiny pieces but Nykola grabbed his wrist. Petro giggled in embarrassment and drew back his hand.

"So much money!" said Granny, in awe. "It must be a land of riches! Did Wasyl Ganczer earn so much in one year?"

Feodor said gruffly, "Better find that agent and get rid of those coins before someone robs you!"

Stefan hurriedly shoved the coins back into the bag. "Yes, I will," he said, replacing the bag inside his blouse. "I heard that he was expected in the next village today. This evening he will be at the tavern there. I want to take Nykola with me and we'll buy our steamship tickets."

Buy our tickets! How grand it sounded! Later, as Nykola walked beside his uncle on their way to see the agent, he could scarcely believe that they were actually going. As they went, Stefan told Nykola all the rumours he had heard about the new land.

"They say the streets of the cities are paved with gold! They say a peasant can become a lord and ride in a carriage!" He turned to Nykola and laughed. "What do you think of that, little lordling?" His nephew merely grinned. "They say there are beautiful young women with heavy necklaces of gold florins just waiting for a man to come along and marry one of them." Suddenly, he shouted as the dancers did in the wedding dance. "Hey! Hey! But I don't believe that!" He danced a few steps in the road. As he twirled, his blue sash fluttered in the air and the coins rattled in the bag.

Laughing, Nykola copied him. He didn't care whether any of the rumours were true. All he wanted was to rejoin his parents, and it seemed that he was going to do that. He danced happily with Stefan.

As suddenly as he had begun, his uncle stopped.

"Come," he said. "We must hurry. We don't want to miss the agent."

On this warm, summer evening, Stefan and Nykola heard the beer drinkers even before they saw the tavern. In front of the low, whitewashed building several men sat on benches singing a sad song about the lost freedom of the Ukraine[6].

Stefan bought a drink and looked carefully around at the people. Men spoke to him and he answered. He even joined in a song. The boy became impatient. Why didn't Uncle find the agent? Didn't he know him? At last, Stefan introduced himself to a young, blond stranger.

Under cover of a loud chorus, Stefan said, "Anton Polanski, I was wondering if you know anything about the steamship companies?"

The young man flashed him a keen look. Quietly, he said, "Were you, Stefan Ganczer?"

"Yes. I was wondering if you were an agent for the steamship company."

"Were you? Were you indeed?"

"Yes."

Nykola began to feel frightened. Had Uncle Stefan spoken to the wrong man?

Without looking directly at Stefan, Anton said, "Steamship agents are not very popular with our Austrian officials, you know."

[6]At the time this story is set, parts of the Ukraine were ruled by the Austro-Hungarian Empire. Ukrainians began to lose their freedom and were forced to learn the Austrian language. They were treated like serfs or slaves.

"Yes! Yes!" Stefan was getting impatient. "I'm not a spy! I want to buy two tickets to take Nykola Ganczer and me to the new land. Are you a ticket agent?"

The stranger looked from Nykola to Stefan and grinned. "If I were, I'd want to see your money before I'd believe you could pay for them."

Stefan flushed. "And if I had the money," he said, "do you think I'd take it out here and let this crowd see it?"

The blond man laughed heartily and lifted his mug to Stefan. He drained it. "I need a refill," he said aloud. Then more quietly, he added, "There's a back room indoors where we can be private."

Stefan grinned. Nykola sighed with relief.

The back room was very small. Stefan and Nykola sat on a bench while the agent pulled out a leather case from under the bed against the other wall. When he sat on the bunk opposite Stefan, their knees almost touched. He raised an eyebrow and Stefan quickly drew out and opened his canvas bag.

"Ah!" said Anton. "Now, you want tickets to the new land?"

"Yes. For Nykola here and myself."

"To what part of the new world?

Brazil? New York? Canada?" He began to pull papers from his bag. "Do you know where you want to go?"

"Yes," exclaimed Nykola. "To Dauphin, Manitoba, in Canada."

Anton laughed and pretended to be astonished. "Well, Stefan Ganczer, I see that your companion does talk. I thought you were taking along a mute."

Nykola felt his face turn red. "My father is in Dauphin, Manitoba, Canada," he said.

"Then, Nykola, little sparrow, you, too, shall go there. But," he said to Stefan, "you understand that I can only sell you a ticket from Lviv to Halifax in Canada."

Stefan looked bewildered. "I don't understand."

"You know where Lviv is?" Anton asked patiently.

"Oh, yes, I once went to the city," Stefan answered.

"Good! Good! Then you must get to Lviv somehow. The first part of the ticket will take you by train to Hamburg. That is the seaport on the Atlantic Ocean. Do you understand?"

"Yes. Hamburg."

"Then at Hamburg you use the next part of your ticket to get on a steamship which will take you across the sea to a city called Halifax, which is in Canada."

Stefan nodded. "Halifax," he repeated.

Nykola was bewildered by all these names he had never heard before. "Is it far from Halifax," he asked, saying it as nearly as possible like the agent had, "to Dauphin?"

Anton Polanski shrugged. "I don't know," he said.

"How do we travel from the seaport to my brother's farm?" asked Stefan.

Again the agent shrugged. "By train, I think. I can sell you a ticket only from Lviv to Halifax."

Stefan frowned. "Will I have enough money to buy two tickets from you as well as train tickets in Canada?"

"Oh, yes. You have a well-stuffed purse. There will be plenty left for travel in Canada." He grinned at Nykola. "To Dauphin, Manitoba, in Canada," he teased.

Nykola grinned back. He didn't mind the teasing. Soon he would be on his way to his own family.

Stefan, too, smiled at the boy. "Then we will buy our tickets," he said.

The agent immediately became businesslike. He selected a form from his case.

"Now," he said briskly, "I must see your passports."

Stefan looked at him blankly. "My passport?"

"Yes. Your passports. It's just to protect me in case you are stopped at the border. The law says I may only sell tickets to people who have passports and come to me of their own free will."

Stefan turned pale. "Passports," he repeated.

Nykola stared at his uncle. For a moment he could not breathe.

"What's wrong?" asked the agent. "Don't you have a passport?"

"No!"

Anton threw the papers back into the case and snapped it shut. "Didn't you know you have to have permission to leave the country?" he asked angrily. "Why do you peasants waste my time? You all want to go to the new land, but you haven't the brains to know how to get there! Well, you can't go without a passport, so get one!"

He stood up and Stefan and Nykola left hurriedly. They didn't speak until they were back on the road to their village.

"What will we do, Uncle?" asked Nykola timidly.

Stefan looked at him blankly for a moment, as if he had forgotten Nykola was with him. "Do?" he asked. "What will we do?" Suddenly, he smiled. "We'll get passports! To leave Austria we must have passports. So, we will get passports."

"Where do we get them, Uncle?"

"I suppose from the administrator of the district. Yes, that must be where we get them. That's where our registration forms and our taxes go. We'll have to go to the Town Hall in Leleshen." He slipped an arm around Nykola's shoulders. "Come, little lordling! Cheer up! We'll get this passport, then buy our steamship tickets and set off to see the new world!"

CHAPTER 3

Stefan's Bad Luck

Nykola lost heart many times during the next ten days, but one morning Stefan ducked under the door frame just as Nykola finished his breakfast.

"Good morning, Feodor Urbanovitch," he said cheerfully. "Good morning, Anna. God be with you, Tetiana Doroshenko." He winked at his nephew. "I have come to take young Nykola with me to get our passports."

"So," said Feodor, "you two fools will try again, will you? It was not fated that you should go to the new land, but fools must find out for themselves."

A frown replaced the smile on Stefan's face. Nykola moved out of Uncle Feodor's reach as if afraid that the man would keep him back by force.

Granny spoke quietly. "If the good God wills it, they will go to the new land. Let the child go with his uncle, Feodor Urbanovitch."

Uncle Feodor shrugged. "He may go for all I care. I can use only one helper today. Petro can come with me to the fields."

Petro made a face at Nykola, but was careful not to let his father see him.

Nykola had never been to the town of Leleshen. Until now, he had travelled only between the village where he grew up and his Uncle Feodor's village. Stefan begged a ride for them in a farm cart taking vegetables to town. Nykola sat among the strong-smelling onions and watched the work going on in the fields they passed. He knew that most peasants farmed two or three acres. He tried to imagine how many of the small fields it would take to equal his father's new homestead. But he could not work it out.

The cart driver was taking his vegetables to the market in the Town Hall square. He showed the building to Stefan and Nykola. They were glad to have a guide because both of them were nervous among the crowds of people in the centre of the town. In the market, farmers and customers bargained loudly with one another. A religious procession came out of a church and crossed the square in front of Nykola and Stefan. After it had passed, they had to step quickly back out of the way of a column of soldiers. The officer barked an order and the soldiers halted, then lounged around the fountain while their officer went into the Town Hall.

Stefan did not seem to want to follow the officer, but Nykola pulled at his sleeve. He wanted to get the passports and go home. Uncle Stefan looked nervously at the soldiers, then climbed up the stairs after Nykola.

Inside, the building was cool and dim. They found a room divided down the middle by a long counter. The army officer stood lounging against it. For a moment, the young man and the boy hesitated.

A clerk called impatiently. "Come! What is it you want?"

Stefan hurried to the counter and explained that they wanted passports. He was showing their registration papers when the officer moved casually over to stand at the clerk's elbow. Nykola stared at the tall soldier whose presence seemed to change the clerk from a bullying lord into a cringing serf.

"Does Your Honour want to see this man's papers?" asked the clerk.

Stefan gasped and reached out for the papers but the officer slowly picked them up and read them through. Nykola's stomach knotted. Little tendrils of fear ran up and down his back. He wanted to look at Uncle Stefan for reassurance, but he could not take his eyes from the soldier's black, pointed mustache.

The officer looked from the papers to the young man.

"Stefan Ganczer, citizen of Austria, nineteen years old, farmhand," he read slowly. "And why do you want a passport?" he asked, sternly.

Stefan tried to answer but no sound came from his dry mouth. Nykola crept close to the counter and leaned against it.

"Thinking of leaving our glorious country, are you?" the officer continued. Still Stefan did not speak. "Answer!"

"Yes, Your Honour!"

Nykola didn't recognize his uncle's voice.

"Never done army service?" barked the officer.

"No, Your Honour."

"Time you did," said the officer briskly. "Clerk, enter this man as enrolled in the army starting today. He'll fill my quota for this district and I can march to the capital tomorrow." He turned to Stefan. "Don't look so stupid! You must know every Austrian has to serve three years in the army!"

"I'm Ukrainian, Your Honour," protested Stefan feebly.

"Ukrainian is Austrian!" said the soldier. "Clerk, show this man my authority to conscript any man who has not done his military service."

Stefan stared stupidly at the paper the trembling clerk thrust in front of him. The officer strode around the counter.

"Come," he said, "you will join my troops outside. We'll send word to your employer."

In a daze, Stefan followed the officer. Nykola crept after them. He paused at the top of the stairs. Blinking in the bright sunshine, he watched the soldiers snap to attention when their officer reappeared. They placed Stefan in the middle of their column.

Nykola brushed his eyes with the sleeve of his blouse and stumbled quickly down the stairs.

"Uncle Stefan!" he cried.

The young man seemed to wake from

a daze. He turned to his nephew. Embracing him closely with one arm, with the other he transferred the canvas bag of coins from inside his own loose tunic to Nykola's.

"Keep it safe," he whispered earnestly. "Go home now."

Nykola's eyes were blinded by tears as he darted into the marketplace crowd. The money bag was heavy. He pulled the sash of his blouse tighter to keep it from falling. Then, afraid the bulge could be seen, he stood with his arms crossed and, from a safe distance, watched Uncle Stefan march off with the soldiers. He turned to find the cart driver beside him.

"What!" he exclaimed. "Have they taken the young man to be a soldier? Just like that?" He looked sympathetically at the little boy. "Well, you didn't expect to leave your uncle in Leleshen, did you now?" Nykola could only shake his head. "Too bad! Shall I give you a ride back? I'm ready to leave."

The kind cart driver took Nykola within a mile of his own village. All the way he cursed and muttered against the Austrian authorities who enslaved the Ukrainian peasants. Nykola never spoke at all. He was too stunned by what had happened.

The family at home, too, were stunned when Nykola stumbled in alone and told his story.

"The money!" demanded Uncle Feodor. "Where's the money?"

"Here," answered Nykola, pulling the bag out of his shirt.

Feodor grabbed the small sack and hugged it to his broad chest. "You did well to keep this from the soldiers!"

As his uncle clutched the money, Nykola suddenly was sure that he would never again see his parents. Uncle Stefan was gone. Uncle Feodor had the money. He choked on the tears that had been threatening since the officer first spoke to Stefan. He must not cry in front of Petro and the rest of the family. Around him, they were discussing the situation over and over again. Granny drew Nykola onto the bench beside her and stroked his hand gently.

"Well, Nykola Ganczer," said Feodor, finally. Nykola gulped down his tears and looked at his uncle. "One thing is sure. You will not now go to the new land. I'll keep this money. You'll have to live here with us. Your father wouldn't expect me to feed you for nothing."

Tetiana Doroshenko straightened her bent back and looked at her son-in-law. "Give me the bag of coins, Feodor Urbanovitch. I will take Nykola to my daughter and her husband."

CHAPTER 4

Running Away

Nykola's head jerked up. Suddenly, his heart was too full. He thought it might burst with hope.

The rest of the family stared at the old lady in amazement.

"Why do you stare as though a dumb woman spoke?" she asked. "I have said that I will take my grandson to the new land and so I shall!"

She was a tiny woman. Her grey head did not reach much above Nykola's as he leaned against her. With black clothes covering her little body and bright eyes darting from Anna to Feodor, she looked like a starling defying a flock of bigger birds.

At first, no one but Nykola took Granny seriously. The next day, when the old woman began to mend clothes for the journey, Anna scolded her mother. "Don't be silly, Tetiana Doroshenko! You can't take the boy. What do you know about making such a long journey?" She talked on, listing all the dangers and hardships of the trip.

Tetiana merely replied mildly, "There is no one else to take him to his parents, so I will take him."

"Go to the priest!" said Anna. "Ask him what you should do."

"There is no need, my daughter. I know what I should do."

"But you have said so many times that you couldn't live without the church! Now you propose to go where there is no church."

Granny sighed deeply. "I shall miss the church. But I said that I could not live without God. God will be with me on the journey and in the new land, just as he is always with me here."

In despair, Anna sent for her mother's sister. She was horrified when she heard what Tetiana intended to do.

"Foolish old woman!" she scolded. "You will not live to the end of such a journey. What good will you do the boy if you die in a foreign land?"

"I know I'm old and unwell," Granny answered. "But God will protect me until I have returned my grandson to his father and mother."

Her sister wailed, "Oh, you will never see our beloved Ukraine again! How can you bear it?"

But nothing moved Granny.

Feodor laughed at the women. "Leave her alone," he said. "You're worrying too soon. She hasn't got a passport yet."

"We will get our passports," replied Granny. "We will go tomorrow morning."

Early the next morning, Granny woke Nykola. "Get ready, Nykola. Today, we are going to get our passports."

Nykola felt both excitement and fear as they set out together after breakfast. He dreaded going back to the Town Hall at Leleshen. What if the clerk recognized him? Granny, too, felt uneasy about facing the officials. She had talked Feodor into giving her one of Wasyl's gold florins and had it changed into smaller coins. Although she did not like to part with hard cash, she had the cunning to know that a bribe would sometimes get you what you wanted. So, Granny made sure that the clerk caught a glimpse of the money under her hand when it rested on the counter. Soon, the clerk had some of the coins and the two travellers were on their way home with their passports.

It was late in the evening when they wearily stumbled into the house. The family were at the dinner table and the delicious smell of cabbage rolls filled the room.

Feodor looked up from his plate. "Here's two more slackers," he said. "The harvest to get in, and where are you two? Off on a wild goose chase after passports! Bah! Is no one around here of any use?"

Granny dropped into a chair. Her feet were burning and her knees aching. She would have liked to close her eyes and rest awhile. But the tone of Feodor's voice warned of trouble. Looking around, she saw Petro lying in a corner.

"Is Petro Urbanovitch hurt?" she asked.

"The clumsy oaf cut himself with a scythe," said his father. Turning to Nykola, who had taken bread for himself and his grandmother, he said, "I hope you intend to earn that bread tomorrow."

"Yes, Uncle," replied Nykola.

He could put up with his uncle's bad temper for a few more days. Soon he would be gone forever!

"While Nykola helps you in the fields, I will go to get the steamship tickets," said

Granny. "So, before you go out in the morning, give me Wasyl's money, Feodor."

Anna put down her glass of tea with a clunk and stared at her mother.

"You don't mean you got the passports?" she asked.

Nykola and Granny exchanged smiles.

"Indeed we did," replied the old woman. "See here!"

She drew the precious papers out of the deep pocket of her skirt.

Uncle Feodor slapped his thigh. "Well," he said, "I never expected you to get them!" He took the papers in his huge hand and turned them back and forth. "So! These papers will allow you to leave the Ukraine, will they?" Suddenly, he laughed. "I know what I should do," he said loudly. Everyone looked at him expectantly. "I should send Petro Urbanovitch away with the old woman and keep Nykola Ganczer here with me. He is worth three of my Petro in the fields."

Nykola's throat tightened. Did his uncle mean that? He looked with frightened eyes at Granny.

She laughed with Feodor. "You wouldn't get me to go then," she said.

"Of course not!" said Anna. "Talk no more such nonsense!"

"You're right," agreed Feodor. "You wouldn't take Petro. Still, he is useless to me with a lame leg. Nykola will have to stay."

"No!" Nykola gasped. "I'm going to the new land!"

Granny's expression warned him to be quiet. To Feodor she said, "You have your daughters to work in the fields. They are as good as Nykola."

"They are now. Some day they'll marry and go off to work for their husbands and what will I do then? Must I hire help? This boy will grow into a strong man. I will keep him here."

Nykola swallowed hard. He must not shout and anger the man further.

"You will not keep him here, Feodor Urbanovitch," said Granny. "He must go to his own family. I will take him."

"Bah!" Feodor stood up and stalked to the door. "You can't go without money. And I have hidden the money Wasyl Ganczer sent."

There was an uncomfortable silence when he had left. Everyone heard Nykola's sob, though he tried to stifle it. Petro snickered.

Anna said crossly, "Go to bed, all of you! Morning comes early."

Tetiana squeezed Nykola's hand as he passed her.

"Don't worry, little quail," she said, softly. "The morning has more wisdom than the evening. I will find a way."

Nykola couldn't sleep. It seemed impossible for Granny to find a way if uncle kept the money. He tossed and turned for what seemed the whole night but was sound asleep when Anna called him early the next morning.

"Hurry! Get up and eat your breakfast. We are all going to the fields today—all except Granny and Petro."

When Granny brought lunch to the workers at noon, she found a chance to talk to Nykola privately. A low stone wall, roughly made, ran along one side of the narrow field. Here, Feodor and his family sat to rest and eat in a small patch of shade made by a lone tree. At a distance, Nykola lay face down in the field. His back was pricked by the sun's heat and his stomach by the stubble.

Granny joined him. "Eat, my son," she said, as she opened a napkin containing his lunch.

"I don't want to eat!" said Nykola, sullenly.

"Don't fret. All will be well. Eat while I

tell you what we will do."

Nykola sat up and accepted the food. "What can we do?" he asked.

"We'll leave tomorrow," Granny whispered.

"But how can we? Uncle won't give you the money."

Granny looked back to where her daughter and son-in-law were resting. "I have the money," she said, very quietly.

Nykola choked on a chunk of bread.

"But Uncle said he hid it!" he exclaimed.

Granny shrugged. "There is only one hiding place in our house and I know where it is. When Petro fell asleep, I took the money and may God forgive me!"

"He will look for it and know you've taken it!"

"No, he thinks we've given up the idea—for now, anyway. He'll not look for the money, yet. But we must go soon. We'll go tomorrow."

Nykola leapt to his feet. "Tomorrow?" he squealed.

"Sh! Sit down!" Granny said, plucking at his red sash.

Nykola looked quickly toward his uncle and sat down close to the old lady.

"How will we find the agent?" he

asked. "Do you know where he is? Uncle will come after us and take back the money."

"Here, eat. They'll wonder what we're talking about." She chewed on a piece of bread before going on. "We can't take time to look for the steamship agent. We'll go to the railway line and get on a train to the seaport. Surely we can buy tickets for the boat there."

Nykola stared at his grandmother in admiration.

"Tomorrow," he repeated. "Will we really go tomorrow?"

"Yes." Granny nodded her head several times. "Now, listen. This afternoon, while you're all at work, I will sew the gold coins into the hem of my skirt and the lining of your jacket. That way they will be safe. Then, I'll pack two bundles for us and hide them behind the big stone in the wall that runs by the road."

"Petro will see you," interrupted Nykola.

"When his father is not standing over him, Petro sleeps. He will not see me. Tomorrow, find out where your uncle will be working. You offer to work somewhere else, somewhere out of his sight. As soon as you can, slip away and meet me by the big stone. You'll not likely be missed until noon and neither will I." She began to fold up the lunch napkins. "There are a lot of carts passing. We'll get a ride and be well away before they know we've gone."

Nykola worked hard all that afternoon, yet hardly knew what he was doing. He thought constantly of his parents and little sisters. He remembered how Olaha used to squeal when he galloped with her on his back. Was he really going to see them all again?

Feodor was in a good mood that night at supper.

"The girls and I can finish the upper field tomorrow," he said. "Nykola, you start cutting the barley in the lower field. When we've finished, we'll come and help you."

"Yes, Uncle," said Nykola.

He kept his eyes down so that Feodor would not see the gladness shining in them. Work alone! Good! That meant he could get away anytime and not be missed.

But, the next day, Nykola found it was not so easy to simply walk away. Several times he told himself that he would put down the scythe at the end of the next row. But each time, he turned back to do

just one more row. Perhaps Granny hadn't had time to get to the road. Nykola didn't want to stand there waiting for her. Perhaps Uncle Feodor would come to see how much work he had done and would catch him running away. Maybe he and Granny would get lost trying to reach the seaport. What if the train crashed? Or the boat sank? Or what if the trip was too much for Granny and she died on the way? What would he say to his mother?

The thought of his mother gave Nykola the necessary courage. Carefully, he wiped the scythe blade and leaned it against a boulder.

Then he ran.

At first, he didn't see Granny at the big stone and his heart sank. As he came closer, he saw someone kneeling on the other side of the wall. With extra clothes under her black dress and a sheepskin coat on top of all, Granny looked almost fat. A babushka was tied over her grey hair so that none of it showed. For a moment, Nykola thought it was his Aunt Anna kneeling there. Then he saw the comforting wrinkles in Granny's face.

He jumped over beside her. She had spread one of her precious, embroidered wedding towels on the ground and was crumbling earth onto it.

"What are you doing, Granny?" asked Nykola.

The old woman looked up at him with tears in her eyes. Slowly and lovingly she wrapped the towel around the earth. Rising stiffly to her feet, she placed the bundle in the big pocket of her skirt.

"I will not be buried in the earth of my beloved country," she said solemnly. "You must see that when I die in the new land, this little piece of the old land is buried with me."

Nykola frowned. Why did Granny talk of dying? Things were bad enough as it was. Uncle Feodor might come looking for them anytime. They should be on their way.

"Come, Granny, we must hurry," he said.

Each picked up one of the bundles. Granny sighed deeply. Nykola helped her over the wall onto the road. Tears still ran down her cheeks.

"What a way to leave!" she wailed. "I have said goodbye to no one. Listen! The church bells! Oh! Oh! I have not asked the priest to bless our journey! May God go with us!"

In a few minutes they had left the village behind. Then the boy, too, felt the old woman's sadness. Nykola felt this moment should be recorded: that on August 30, 1900, Tetiana Doroshenko and Nykola Ganczer left their village in the Ukraine, never to return.

CHAPTER 5

"You Can't Go to Canada"

Nykola and Granny had only walked a short distance when a cart stopped to pick them up. It was full of young women going to help with the potato harvest on an estate. The girls were curious about their bundles, but Granny soon had them chattering about their own affairs instead. Next, a sullen young man gave them a ride in an empty hayrack. He told them none of his business and asked them none of theirs.

The oxen, so slow and plodding, suddenly shied, and Nykola sat up in surprise. When the driver had them under control, Nykola asked what had happened to frighten them. The man pointed with his whip to a long, freight train coming nearer and nearer.

The hayrack reached the track before the last cars had passed. Everything about the train thrilled Nykola—the size and power of the engine, the shriek of the whistle and the clickety-clack of the wheels, the plume of smoke and the swaying of the cars. He stood grasping the bars of the hayrack, holding himself down, for he felt like leaping into the air in his excitement. No longer was he sad or afraid. He wanted to board the train and go on and on forever. He turned to Granny and found her eyes shining with excitement, too. They laughed at one another.

Granny asked the young man, "Where can we get on a passenger train?"

"There's a station just a mile down the track," he answered in a flat voice.

Nykola threw the two bundles off the wagon, jumped to the ground and turned to help Granny down.

"Thank you!" Nykola called.

"God be with you!" said Granny.

Walking on the railway ties was difficult and it seemed to Nykola that they went very slowly. He had time to remember his uncle and to wonder whether he had missed them yet. Would he come after them? Nykola hoped there would be a train soon to take them far beyond Uncle Feodor's reach.

The station consisted of a platform and

a shack with a bench against the wall. Four people were gathered outside the building. Granny and Nykola stood on the edge of the platform and watched in silence for several minutes. A man came along, went up to the window in the shack, and said the name of a town. He placed money on the counter and in exchange, received a ticket.

"What is the name of the seaport?" Granny asked.

"Hamburg," answered Nykola.

"Hamburg," she repeated.

She reached deep into her pocket and took out a gold piece. Followed closely by Nykola, she timidly approached the window, looked up at the clerk behind the counter and said, "Hamburg."

The clerk, a fat man with hairy chest and arms, glanced up at them.

"How many?" he asked.

"Two."

"One way or return?" Seeing Granny staring blankly, he snapped, "One way or return? Are you coming back?"

Granny shook her head firmly.

"No!" she said.

Behind her, Nykola echoed, "No!"

"Two singles to Hamburg," the clerk muttered over and over to himself as he pawed through the pages of a tattered railway schedule. Finally, he slapped two long tickets onto the counter and stamped them several times. Keeping his hands on the tickets, he repeated aloud, "Two singles to Hamburg." Granny laid down a gold coin. He scooped it up with one dirty hand while he pushed the tickets and some small change toward her with the other.

"Change trains at the border," he said abruptly.

"Change? Why?" asked Granny, timidly.

"Because the train doesn't go any farther," the fat man said, scornfully. He turned away.

Granny picked up the tickets and held them out to Nykola. With one finger, he reached out and touched them. He grinned at her and she smiled back. Then, they sat on the edge of the platform and settled themselves to wait. Granny pulled a small loaf of bread out of her pocket and shared it with her grandson. Hardly had they finished eating, when they heard the train whistle and saw it slowly pulling into the station. Hurriedly, they gathered their bundles.

They found a coach that was almost

empty and Nykola stowed their two bundles under a seat. Nykola felt a rush of excitement as the train pulled out of the station. Everything interested him—his fellow passengers, the speed at which they moved through the countryside, the little fields where people were working at the harvest. How surprising to be here, riding in a train, instead of doing just what those peasants were doing! After a while, he was astonished to see that Granny had fallen asleep. How could she sleep when there was so much to see? Soon, however, the stifling heat of the coach and the motion of the train put him to sleep also.

He awakened when the train stopped with a jerk and the conductor threw open the door.

"Border point!" he shouted. "All out! Bring your baggage! Have your passports ready!"

Ever since the day Uncle Stefan had been taken away to be a soldier, the word 'passport' frightened Nykola. Now, waking from an uneasy doze to hear the word being shouted by a man in uniform, he was terrified. Granny patted his shoulder and he followed her off the train and into a shed-like building. An official announced that they would be here for an hour while all the passports and baggage were checked.

The smell of cooking came from a canteen at one end of the building. Suddenly, Nykola realized how hungry he was. It was evening now, and except for the bread he had munched on the station platform, he had not eaten since breakfast in Uncle Feodor's house. How long ago that seemed!

Granny handed him a few coins.

"Go and buy hot soup for us, Nykola," she said. "I'll get out some bread."

Nykola stood in line and saw the man ahead of him put down one kopek and receive two bowls of soup. So, he put down one kopek and asked for two bowls.

"Have you another kopek?" demanded a huge woman, with spoon upraised.

"Yes," the boy answered.

"It's two kopeks," she said.

Nykola did not dare to protest so he paid and carried the soup safely to Granny, in spite of his trembling hands.

The old woman was shocked when she heard what he had paid for it.

"They're robbers!" she said. "We'll soon have no money."

More money went to bribe the official who stamped their passports and the customs man who allowed them into Germany. The stop had been costly, but when the next train slowly pulled out of the Ukraine, Granny looked at Nykola with a twinkle in her eye.

"Feodor Urbanovitch has no passport," she said.

"No," agreed Nykola, laughing back at her.

They settled themselves to sleep through the night.

Very early the next morning, the train drew into the huge, busy station in the seaport of Hamburg. The Ukrainian peasants from Nykola's coach all stood huddled together on the platform. Steam engines hissed, loudspeakers crackled, porters and conductors shouted, and people talked in different languages. All the sounds rose together to the glass roof high overhead and echoed back. Everywhere, people were moving among piles of luggage.

A station policeman came toward the group, gesturing and shouting. Although they didn't understand a word he said, they followed him like sheep up the stairs into the waiting room. Never had Nykola imagined any building as huge as this! Could the Czar's palace be so grand?

The policeman herded them over to a Travellers' Aid booth. A woman explained to them, in Ukrainian, that they could get beds at the emigration shed near the waterfront. But, at the shed, harrassed officials waved them away, saying the places were all filled.

"But where are we to go?" asked a young woman with a baby in her arms.

"There are boarding houses in the streets nearby," was the answer. "You must try one of them."

Nykola and Granny, each carrying a bundle, set off along the busy streets. Everything was strange to them. Heavy wagons rolled over cobblestones almost

drowning out the hum of hundreds of voices. The smell of the sea mingled with the odours of the cargoes the ships were loading and unloading. Instead of rows of separate, one-storey, whitewashed houses, such as they were used to in their village, here were tall brick and wooden buildings built one beside the other, many of them with the upper levels overhanging the street and shutting out the sky. Some of the ground floor premises were shops but the names over the doors were in German and meant nothing to Nykola. To Granny, it did not matter because she could not read.

For a time, they wandered aimlessly. Often, they were jostled by impatient people so that they were forced off the sidewalk into the filthy road. Then, frightened by a clattering cart, they would leap back onto the sidewalk. At last, Nykola saw a sign in Ukrainian. BEDS, it read. They stepped into the narrow, dark hallway where the heat and smell were even worse than in the streets.

A woman's head and shoulders appeared at an opening in one wall. She stared at them crossly for a moment and then spoke in Ukrainian.

"What do you want?"

Granny was delighted to hear her own language.

"Can we stay here?" she asked, with a smile.

"Have you money?"

"Yes."

"Just the two of you?"

"Yes."

"There's a small room you can have. Space for two to sleep and you can cook in the kitchen downstairs. One florin a week and you pay a week in advance."

Granny gasped. "A whole florin! But we won't be here a week. We're going to Canada."

"Pay a week in advance or no room. Suit yourself."

The woman waited at the window.

Granny muttered to herself, looked at her weary grandson, glanced out the door and finally said, "We'll stay."

The landlady led them up a dirty flight of stairs. She unlocked the door of a tiny, windowless room. It was furnished with two straw mattresses, a rickety wooden chair and a small table. On the table stood a tin washbasin and a candle stub in a battered, tin candlestick.

"You want the candle?" asked the woman indifferently.

Granny looked round the dark cubby-hole and nodded.

"Two kopeks extra."

She held out her hand and waited in silence while Tetiana drew out a gold coin. Immediately, her manner became friendlier. She gave Granny the key.

"Lock your bundles in the room. I'll show you the kitchen."

They followed her down to the gloomy cellar and were shown a stove, a large, dirty table, and several benches.

"You can use the table and the cooking pots, but you supply your own dishes. Don't have any? Buy them at the shop on the corner. You'll need them on the ship. Have to supply your own utensils there, you know. There's always hot water." She pointed to a huge copper boiler. "You can cook at five o'clock every day."

The long, exhausting day had finally ended. Together, Granny and Nykola knelt before the icon[7] while the old woman prayed. Then they lay down on the hard beds. Fleas in the mattresses, rustlings in the walls, and their own thoughts kept them awake. Granny was frightened at the speed with which their money was disappearing. They had already used several florins and they

[7] ī'kon a sacred picture

hadn't yet bought the steamship tickets. Nykola, on the other hand, was excited by the thought that, in the morning, they were really going to board a ship for Canada. When he did fall asleep, he dreamed that his father and mother and two little sisters were waiting on the dock when the ship pulled in, but he couldn't get off the boat to reach them.

In the kitchen next morning, they met a kindly Ukrainian woman who was going with her family to New York. She had been waiting a week for a ship and was able to give them the information they needed. Following her advice, they went back to the waterfront and found the offices of the steamship companies, and the immigration agents of many different countries.

Nykola found the Canadian immigration agent, and he and Granny joined a scraggly line-up in front of his desk. That morning, Granny had ripped open her dress hem and taken out more of the precious, gold coins. She sat on her bundle, fingering them nervously as the line moved forward.

Nykola could not sit still. He talked to anyone who looked Ukrainian, then brought back news to Granny.

"There's a boat going to Canada tomorrow!...The boat is going to Halifax.... When we get to Halifax, we must go on a very long, train journey to Dauphin. Even longer than to Hamburg!...On the boat, we'll have our food served to us; you won't have to cook!"

Granny smiled at him each time and by the time they reached the desk, she was almost as excited as he was. The agent wore a uniform and an intimidating military mustache and side whiskers. Nykola and Granny stood waiting for him to arrange his papers. After a long time, he looked up. He addressed them in German, but at their blank looks he switched to Ukrainian.

"Names?" he asked, briskly.

"Tetiana Doroshenko and Nykola Ganczer."

"Just two of you?"

"Yes."

The agent put down his pencil and folded his hands.

"What age are you?" he asked Granny.

"Fifty-six."

"And the boy?"

"I am ten years old," answered Nykola.

The man pursed his lips as he looked from one to the other. Then he picked up his papers, straightened them by tapping them on the desk and shook his head firmly.

"No. Sorry. You can't go to Canada. Old women and small boys aren't wanted there," he said.

CHAPTER 6

Granny Finds a Way

Nykola wanted to cry out, "My family is in Canada! My father sent us money to go to him."

If only he had, all would have been well. The immigration man thought Granny and Nykola were going to add two more to the number of destitute people arriving weekly in Canada. If he had known that they had someone to support them, he would have signed their papers.

But, Nykola was too stunned and Granny too frightened to speak up. The look of bitter disappointment in the little boy's eyes shamed the man and made him speak gruffly.

"Move along, now," he said. "Next!"

Granny and Nykola were shoved away from the desk. Bewildered and unhappy,

Granny headed for the door. Nykola pulled her back.

"No, Granny," he said. "No! Don't go! We have to go to Canada."

Tetiana turned and took his hand. She shook her head gently. All around them people were intent on their own business. No one seemed to notice their distress. Together, they retreated to a corner.

"Granny, what can we do?"

"Hush, Nykolenko! We must think."

The old woman sat down heavily on her bundle. Nykola crouched beside her, staring hopefully into her face. When she said nothing, he gradually sank down and looked idly about him. There were many families in the room. Most had young children with them—several much younger than Nykola—and a few had grandparents. If they could go, why couldn't he and Granny?

"If we were with our family," he said slowly, "it would be all right. Lots of old women and children are going."

Granny looked silently at all the people waiting patiently. Then she struggled to her feet.

"Come, Nykola. We'll return to the boarding house."

"No, Granny, I don't want to go back to

the boarding house! I want to get on a ship!"

"Don't fret, my little Nykola. I've thought of a way."

Although he did not understand, Nykola followed her in complete trust. It was only mid-morning when they arrived back at the house. Just as they reached the door, a small boy in a butcher's apron leaped through it followed by the landlady, shouting in German and waving her stout, bare arms. At the corner, safely out of reach, the boy stopped and stuck out his tongue. Hannah Pawlicky shook a huge fist at him. Nykola grinned behind her back, but sobered quickly when she turned to him and Granny.

Still using her loudest voice, she said, "And how have you got on then, Tetiana Doroshenko? Will you be leaving tomorrow?"

"Yes," lied Tetiana. "You will soon rent the room again," she added pleasantly, "with so many travellers in the city."

The woman nodded and they followed her into the house. Before she disappeared into her own room, Granny said, "I saw another family arrive yesterday evening. They were Ukrainian, weren't they?"

"Yes! A lazy lot!" she answered. "In the kitchen now. Slept till nine and still at their breakfast!"

Granny made sympathetic noises and led Nykola downstairs. There were three people sitting at the bare wooden table, drinking tea from tin cups. A strong smell of salted fish suggested what they had eaten, although that smell seemed to be everywhere in Hamburg and might have lingered from some former meal in this airless room.

Nykola looked carefully at the family. The woman resembled Aunt Anna except that she was even fatter. She had the same anxious look. The man was short and slight, with light-coloured hair and beard. He reminded Nykola of the school teacher back home. But the teacher had always worn an open, friendly expression. This face was cunning, and the man's first glance at Granny and Nykola was full of suspicion.

Tetiana smiled and introduced herself and her grandson. The newcomers were Josef Koumka, his wife, Vera Barsky, and their daughter, Daria. Daria was older than Nykola—about fifteen, he judged, comparing her to Uncle Feodor's oldest daughter.

Granny began to talk to them in a friendly, sympathetic way and the family soon began to tell her about themselves. Daria was behind the move to the new land. She wanted to follow her sweetheart there. They had very little money. Having got as far as the seaport, Josef had no definite plans for going farther. It was all going to cost so much, he said. How did his daughter know life would be better across the sea? As for him, he had always found life hard; luck was always against him. He expected that it would be just the same wherever he went.

"All the same, Father," said Daria, "we are going."

"Ah, yes," answered Josef, "we'll go. There's nothing for us here in Hamburg. As well go on as go back."

If Granny had had a choice, she would not have asked this family to help her. But with the ship sailing tomorrow, she couldn't take time to look for anyone else. She told Josef about Wasyl Ganczer, who had gone out to Canada just fifteen months ago and had a large farm already. He had even made enough money working for the railroad to send for his son.

"Is it so, Tetiana Doroshenko?" asked

Vera. Her double chin trembled with eagerness. "You see, Husband, how well a man may do in this new country."

"Just think, Father, you, the owner of such a farm!"

"Ah, ah," answered Josef, wagging his head. "I've heard many fantastic stories of this new land. When I see it, I'll believe it."

"A boat sails for Canada tomorrow," said Granny.

"Tomorrow? Oh, Father, we must take it!"

But Josef did not like to be rushed.

"We'll see. We'll see, Daughter," he said.

There was a silence. Daria pouted. Vera looked anxious. Granny drew out a gold coin and casually tapped the table with it. All three of them stared at it.

"My grandson and I want to go on that boat," Granny said. She explained what the immigration officer had said to them that morning. "We saw many old women and little boys who were going. They were part of a family. If we had gone with Wasyl Ganczer and my daughter, there would have been no difficulty. You see our problem. We must have a family to travel with." She laid the coin on the table.

"Wasyl Ganczer sent us an extra florin in addition to our passage money. If we could find a family who would take us with them, we would gladly pay them this gold coin."

Josef scratched his neck behind the ear.

"Well, now, Granny," he said, "as you know, we are going to Canada. Why couldn't we go on this boat tomorrow and take you along as part of our family?"

Nykola wanted to shout for joy. Granny remained calm and spoke quietly.

"That would be good of you, Josef Koumka." She pushed the coin toward him and nodded to the two women. "We would be happy to travel with you."

Just as Josef's hand closed over the gold piece, the landlady clattered into the kitchen. She scolded them for taking so long over their meal.

The three women finally got Josef on his way to the waterfront. They made a little procession as they walked. Nykola led the way. After him came the farmer and his wife, and then their daughter and Tetiana. Inside the shed, there were more people than ever. Nykola was glad to see that there were now two men at the Canadian immigration office. Word had got around Hamburg that a ship would sail for Halifax and both officers were very busy.

Nykola was steering the Koumka family toward the second Canadian officer when Josef was hailed by another Ukrainian peasant. They all turned aside. Nykola kicked a wooden trunk in frustration.

After an exchange of greetings, the friend said, "We're off to Brazil!"

"And we to Canada," answered Josef.

"Canada! Ah, you're making a mistake! Why go where there's ice and snow nearly all the year? Brazil is warm. Crops grow all the time. Besides, what do they give you in Canada?"

"Free land! One hundred and sixty acres just for the asking!" answered Josef.

His friend tapped him on the chest, a look of triumph on his face. "I'm getting twice that in Brazil! Do they pay your passage?"

"No! Do you mean to say you get free passage?"

"Yes, free passage out for my whole family and free land when I get there!"

Josef turned to his wife. "Do you hear that? A free passage out." He scratched behind his ear. "That would give us more money for a start."

Vera's double chins folded into one another as she nodded her head thoughtfully.

"Yes," she agreed. "The steamship tickets will cost a lot. It would be a saving."

Nykola exchanged a look of despair with Granny.

Their friend said, "We have been promised a cow and a loan to buy tools. Oh, I tell you, Brazil is the place!"

"You may be right," said Josef, slowly.

Much to Nykola's relief, Daria spoke up.

"I have heard that Brazil is a very hot country. Our people get sick in the jungle and die of fever. Don't you remember, Father? The overseer told how many hundreds of Ukrainian peasants died in Brazil. Canada is healthier."

"Ho, ho," laughed her father, "we all know why you want to go to Canada!"

"A sweetheart," explained Vera and all the adults laughed at the blushing girl.

"All the same," interrupted Granny, "Canada is more like our own land. We'll all feel more at home there."

"That's right," said another Ukrainian who had been eavesdropping. "Before you can farm in Brazil, you have to clear the jungle. That's hard work. In Canada, the land is all clear. You just plow, plant your seed, and wait for the crop to grow!"

Josef turned to him. "Are you sure?" he asked.

"Sure as I'm standing here! My brother settled in Canada and that's what he wrote to me. I'm going out to join him." He spoke to the man who was going to Brazil. "I'll get my free land and take off my first crop before you have the jungle cleared from your land."

He was a big man with a loud voice and hearty laugh. He inspired confidence. Josef looked at him thoughtfully.

"You may be right," Josef said.

"Of course, I'm right! Canada's the place for you! Why break your back clearing the jungle when you can have rich, black loam all ready to grow a crop?" He winked at Nykola who was smiling up at him. "Have you got your tickets? Better get them. The ship sails tomorrow!"

Josef made up his mind, said goodbye to his friend, and wished him the best of luck in Brazil. Sighing with relief, Granny and Nykola followed him to the desk of the Canadian officer. With no trouble, Josef obtained entry papers for all five of them. Then he bought the tickets. On the passenger list, Granny became Tetiana Doroshenko, mother of Josef Koumka and her grandson became Nykola Koumka. They were told to report to the dock early the next morning for a medical examination, after which they would be allowed to board the ship.

At last, thought Nykola. At last, he and Granny had their steamship tickets! It wouldn't be long now till he was with his own family again. How surprised they would be to see him with Granny instead of Uncle Stefan!

CHAPTER 7

Goodbye to the Old Country

Nykola and Granny went with the Koumkas to buy the things they would need on the ship, then they went back to their room to rest. By the time they reached the top of the stairs, Granny was trembling with fatigue. She dropped thankfully onto the chair.

"Are you all right, Granny?" asked Nykola anxiously.

"It's just the excitement," she told him. "Too much worry. But we've done well. We have the tickets. Still, I'll be glad when we're on board that ship. I wish we didn't have to trust Josef Koumka. He's lazy and crafty. We haven't much money left. If we don't get on that ship tomorrow, I don't know what will become of us."

There was a knock on the door. The landlady stepped in and closed the door behind her. To Granny, she said, "Light the candle. I want to talk to you."

Granny obeyed with trembling hands. In the flickering light, the woman looked sinister. What now? thought Nykola.

"You owe me another week's rent for the room," said Hannah.

"But we're going tomorrow. I told you that."

"Maybe so, but still, Tetiana Doroshenko, I think you will pay me another florin."

"No!" Granny clasped her hands tightly in her lap so that her arms were pressed against the pockets of her skirt.

Hannah, moving a step nearer, seemed to tower over little Tetiana. In a hard voice she said, "No doubt the immigration officials would be interested in the deal I overheard you make with Josef Koumka."

"Another florin! We'll have no money left!" groaned Granny. "Please, Hannah Pawlicky, have pity! I must have money to take my grandson to his parents in Canada. I can't afford to pay you any more."

The other woman shrugged. "Suit yourself. It will cost you more than that to go back to the Ukraine."

"No! We can't go back!"

"Well, they won't let you go to Canada if they know you lied to them."

Granny was trembling with anger and despair.

"Robber!" she hissed. "Cheat!"

Hannah's expression never changed. "I've been called worse," she said, holding out her hand.

"And deserved it," said the old woman bitterly.

Nevertheless, she grudgingly handed out the money.

That night, the boy slept fitfully. Once when he awoke, he saw that Granny had lit the candle and was sitting before it with her icon propped on the candlestick. From the floor, her shadow looked huge and he wondered if it was part of his nightmare. Then he heard her groan. Frightened, he called out to her.

"Go to sleep, little Nykola," she answered.

"But, what is it, Granny? Are you sick?"

He remembered the day in his uncle's house when Tetiana's sister had come to try to persuade her not to go to the new land. She had said that Granny wouldn't live to the end of such a journey. Was it true? Nykola wanted to jump up and run to the old lady, but he was too scared to move.

"Are you sick, Granny?" he asked again.

"No, no, Nykolenko." She raised her head with an effort and tried to smile. "Don't worry. It's nothing. I'm just excited. And too tired to sleep. What a time we have had, my Nykola! So much worry and excitement!" Her voice became stronger. "Here we are at the seaport! We'll sail away tomorrow. Don't worry, little quail. Go to sleep."

Nykola crept over and grasped her rough hands.

"Oh, Granny, you can't be sick! Not now! Please, don't take the fever!" he pleaded, remembering that terrible day when he had awakened from his sickness to find that his family had gone away and left him behind.

Granny carried his hand to her cheek.

"No, no. See? My cheek is cool. I have no fever." She smiled at him. "The good God will preserve me till I have taken you to your mother. Go back to bed, little quail, and sleep. We must be up early."

Next morning, they were among the last to arrive at the dockside because Josef could not be hurried. It was a warm, bright day so a section of the dock near the *Atlantic Queen* had been roped off for the steerage passengers. The doctor, his assistant, and an interpreter stood beside a table and examined each passenger.

With the doctor speaking in German, and the interpreter in Ukrainian almost at the same time, Nykola automatically obeyed the commands.

"Open your mouth! Wide! Is your throat sore? Open your shirt! Any rash? Been sick lately? No? Good! Move on. Next!"

It took about three minutes for all five of them to be passed by the doctor.

As soon as the medical examinations were over, the rope barrier was removed and the immigrants began to stream up to the deck of the ship. At the top of the gangplank, a young man took Granny's elbow and steadied her as she stepped down. He was an interpreter hired by the steamship company to travel with the steerage passengers. Nykola jumped down beside Granny. They exchanged grins as they felt the deck of the *Atlantic Queen* beneath their feet. Now they were really on their way to Dauphin, Manitoba, Canada.

When everyone was aboard, the interpreter led them all down below into a long, low room in the hold.

Down the middle of the room, a row of tables and benches was fastened to the floor. On both sides hung rows of three-tiered bunks, also bolted to the ship. Women and girls were directed to one side of the hold and men and boys to the other. Granny, like other older women, was given a lower bunk. Vera Barsky was next to her and Daria above her mother. Opposite them, Nykola took the top bunk, with Josef under him. To Nykola's delight, the man who had helped to persuade Josef not to go to Brazil was at the bottom of their tier. He had no family with him.

Because there was so little room in which to move, there was a great deal of noise and confusion as people tried to get settled in the tiny space that was to be home for more than a week. Nykola spread his blanket and pillow on the lumpy straw mattress and hung his coat, cap, extra shirt, and boots on a nail. On the little box-like shelf he placed his mug, plate, knife, and spoon. He dived under the table to Granny's bunk and found that she had done the same except that, in addition, she had hung her icon from a nail in the wall.

"Let's go up on deck, Granny," said Nykola. "I want to see us leave."

The old woman threw up her hands.

"No, no, Nykolenko! Indeed I couldn't. I'm so thankful to be sitting down. I couldn't climb those stairs right now. Nothing but a ladder! I'll just stay here."

"But, Granny, don't you want to see the ship sail?"

"Ho, little sparrow," came a booming voice from the opposite side, "I'll go with you. I want to see the last of old Europe." It was the man whose bunk was under Josef's. "My name is Ivan Tabaka, Granny," he said. "I'll keep an eye on the youngster and see he doesn't fall overboard. Let him come with me."

Granny nodded her consent and Nykola met the man at the foot of the stairs.

"Isn't your father coming?" asked Ivan.

"My father?" For a moment Nykola was puzzled. Then he remembered that he was supposed to be Josef's son. "No," he answered. "He's. . .he's not ready."

He pointed to where Josef was sitting on his bunk waiting for his wife to come and spread his blanket for him.

Many other passengers went up and the rail was soon crowded. It was a dazzlingly bright day. In the city, the heat was oppressive, but here at the waterfront a breeze cooled the air a little. Nykola and his friend were in time to hear the order given to cast off. There was one prolonged blast of the whistle and Nykola saw the dock slipping slowly past and a gap widening between the ship and the shore. The *Atlantic Queen* was on its way to Halifax.

As Nykola looked up and down the railing, he saw that many of the older people were crying. But he didn't feel sad at all. He was glad! Glad to be away from Uncle Feodor, away from the officials who stole Uncle Stefan from him, and away from Hamburg. And glad to be going to his own family in the new land.

Nykola felt his friend's hand on his shoulder. He looked up into the man's face. It was serious but not sorrowful.

"May God prosper us in the land we are going to," said Ivan Tabaka.

CHAPTER 8

The Stolen Blanket

That evening, at their first meal on board, the steerage passengers found out just how crowded their quarters were. There was not nearly enough room at the table for everyone. Josef and his wife and daughter found places for themselves; Ivan gave his up to Granny and Nykola. He and many others sat on the lower bunks with their plates in their laps. Three sailors served the meal. One carried a big, iron pot from which a second ladled a portion of hot mush onto each plate. Following them, the third sailor added a chunk of hard bread from a sack hanging at his waist.

Water rationing was the responsibility of the interpreter, Dymtro Malkovitch. He explained to each family group that the water had to last through the voyage and, therefore, they could only have what he gave them. When he heard the speech,

Ivan good-naturedly suggested that the seats at the table had better be rationed, too.

Dymtro only laughed. "There'll be plenty of seats tomorrow," he said.

"Why?" asked Ivan.

"Seasickness," answered the interpreter.

Breakfast next morning proved him right. Almost all the adults stayed on their bunks when the sailors came in with the same hot mush, hard bread, and water. Granny and Josef were both sick. Granny would eat nothing; Josef sipped a little water from the cup his wife held to his lips.

Nykola sat at the table and made a face at the food. Beside him, Ivan ate steadily. He grinned at Nykola.

"Eat, my young friend," he said. "I have learned one thing in my life—eat when you can. Often enough you'll go hungry."

Nykola swallowed a few mouthfuls. He felt he would choke in the foul air. There was no ventilation in the cabin. Some people had been sick all night and many more were being sick all around him.

Ivan Tabaka looked at the white faces

of Nykola and the other children. He called the interpreter.

"Ho, Dymtro Malkovitch, can we take these children up on deck? They need fresh air."

Dymtro shook his head. "The sailors don't like them up there. They get in the way."

"We could keep them out of the sailors' way. See that fellow there who played the accordion last night? Ask him to come up on deck. We'll get the youngsters dancing. Fresh air and exercise, too," he said.

Dymtro spoke in German to the accordion player and then went off to seek permission from the captain. Ivan had the children lined up when he returned.

"Yes, you may go," he reported. "But the children must stay behind the rope."

"Good!" said Ivan. He clicked his heels together. "Attention! Forward march!"

Few of the children understood his words, but they all understood his actions and they followed him eagerly. Nykola looked doubtfully at Granny. He longed to go up on deck. Should he stay with the sick woman?

Vera Barsky called to him, "You go, young Nykola. You can't help her. I'll do what is necessary."

"Thank you, Auntie," said Nykola. He scrambled up the ladder to the fresh, clean air.

Ivan soon had the children organized. Nykola was proud of his big countryman. Under his guidance, the steerage children spent most of the daylight hours on deck throughout the voyage. Thus, they stayed healthy in spite of the fact that from supper time till after breakfast, all were shut up together in the foul hold with its bad air, overcrowding, and darkness.

Fortunately, the weather remained good and the sea relatively calm. Most of the seasick victims recovered quickly. Granny did not leave her bunk for three days. Nykola was very worried about her. Without food, she seemed to grow weaker and smaller before his eyes. Sometimes her mind wandered and she thought she was back home.

One day, while Josef was still spending the day on his bunk, Nykola went as usual to Granny's side when he came down for dinner at noon. Although her bed was in shadow, her eyes seemed clear and bright as she peered up at him.

"Nykola," she whispered urgently, "bring me your coat."

"My coat? Why, Granny?"

"Never mind why! Do as I say! Get your coat!"

Nykola wondered if Granny's mind was wandering again. He climbed up to his bunk, lifted the coat from the nail, and carried it to Tetiana.

With trembling hands, she ran her fingers along the hemline. She sighed with relief. Pulling Nykola close to her, she spoke in a low voice, "You must wear your coat all the time."

"But, Granny, I don't need it!"

"Nevertheless, you must wear it! This morning I saw Josef take down your coat when he thought I was sleeping. I called out to him and he put it back. But another time I may not see him. He's after the coins." She raised her head and looked across the hold. "We must have money when we get to Halifax," she said, dropping back onto the pillow. "You know it is said to be a long way from the seaport to your father's farm. What would we do without money? Guard your coat carefully!"

"Yes. Yes, I will," Nykola answered.

He was frightened. He and Granny were so alone. Very few of the people on the ship even spoke their language and they all had families of their own to care for. Except Ivan. He had no family. And he was certainly friendly. Perhaps he would be their protector.

From then on, Nykola spent as much time as he could with Ivan, who was always kind to him.

One day, when it was time for the children to go below again, Ivan steered Nykola into a corner behind a smoke stack. Dymtro, the interpreter, joined them in a few minutes. Nykola felt proud to be allowed to join the young men as they talked. Dymtro told them that he was working on the ship to earn money to go to university. He wanted to be a teacher or a lawyer.

"That's fine for you," said Ivan. "A man with brains should use them. As for me, I'll be a farmer. My brother left the Ukraine a poor man, just two years ago. Now, he has a big farm, some cattle, a wife, even a baby—or maybe two by this time. Yes, that's the life for me. Just let them give me my free land."

Dymtro smiled at this enthusiasm. "Where is your brother's farm?"

"In the Ukrainian colony near Edmonton. Do you know it?"

"No, I've never been there, but many passengers are headed for there. They tell me it is a large and prosperous colony."

"That's the place for me," said Ivan, grinning at Nykola. "Oh, won't I give them a surprise when I turn up at the door?"

"Don't they expect you?" asked Nykola.

"No, no, they think I'm still back in Austria. What a surprise they'll get!"

Suddenly, he flushed and looked away from Dymtro and Nykola. He seemed embarrassed about something.

Nykola was puzzled. Why wasn't Ivan's brother expecting him? He must have written letters or how would Ivan know so much about him? Why hadn't Ivan written to him? Could Ivan have run away the way he and Granny had? No, of course not! Ivan was...well, Ivan wouldn't have an Uncle Feodor bossing him around!

Before they could ask him more questions, Ivan began to imitate what his brother and his brother's wife and even the baby would do when they saw him.

Nykola laughed with delight. It was all so much as he had imagined his own family would act.

"Yes, yes!" he said, "That's just what my mother will say when she sees me and

Granny. She thinks Uncle Stefan will be with me. They thought we were going in the spring. They don't even know Granny and I are on the way! My father..." Suddenly, he realized what he was saying.

There was an awkward silence. Ivan broke it.

"I knew Josef Koumka and Vera weren't your parents," he said gently. "Don't worry. I won't give you away."

Then, Ivan looked enquiringly at the interpreter. After all, he was an official of sorts. He might feel it was his duty to report the boy and his grandmother.

But Dymtro shook his head. "I won't tell," he said. "How did it happen you're with the Koumkas?"

Nykola poured out the whole story to his two friends.

He told Granny about it later. She said he was foolish to have told their secret.

"They'll never give us away," declared Nykola.

Still, there was something of a mystery about Ivan. He was always talking and yet he told nothing about himself except that he was going to his brother's farm. He had even less baggage than Granny and Nykola. Although he was always urging others to go to the captain with their grievances, he never spoke to any of the ship's officers or even to the sailors.

After Nykola had confessed that Josef wasn't his father, Ivan openly expressed his contempt for the lazy fellow.

"One day Josef Koumka is going to be sorry if he doesn't stop grumbling," he said with a grin. "I'll hang him by his pants from the lantern hook and we'll see who helps him down!"

One evening, Nykola thought he was going to see Josef put in his place. As he was getting ready for bed, he saw in the dim light that Josef had Ivan's boots on his bed. Ivan saw them, too.

"Ho, Josef Koumka," said Ivan in an unnaturally loud voice, "do you think you can fill my boots? And you such a little man?"

In the darkness, Nykola grinned expectantly.

"Maybe I couldn't fill them," came Josef's thin voice, "but if they were lost, I could claim them as well as you. See these initials? Do they stand for Ivan Tabaka?" Ivan glared at the small man. Josef spoke very softly as he examined the boots with care. "Good thick boots, Ivan Tabaka. Very like the ones the Austrian army issues, aren't they? Not your initials, though.

Now, I wonder. Where did you get these boots?"

Nykola could not see Josef, who was sitting on the bunk beneath him, but he had a good view of Ivan's face and he was surprised to see his friend turn pale. Instead of roaring at Josef and hanging him from the lantern hook as he had threatened to do, Ivan snatched the boots from Josef without a word and rolled onto his own bed. Nykola frowned. Why did Ivan let Josef get away with that?

In the next moment, Nykola wondered whether he had any friends at all. He had just climbed up into his bunk after saying good night to his grandmother, when he saw that his blanket was gone. Perhaps Granny had taken it. He called out to her, but she said she didn't have it. Worried now, he went to Dymtro and told him that his blanket was missing.

The interpreter frowned.

"Stolen, I suppose," he said.

Granny joined them. "You must get it back, Dymtro Malkovitch," she said.

The young man shrugged. "How am I to do that?"

"Find out who stole it and make him give it back," demanded Granny.

"Can I accuse a whole ship of theft?

During every voyage there is much thievery. I can't stop it. You must learn to protect your own property."

As he turned to walk away, Tetiana clutched his sleeve.

"A blanket I wove myself!" she said. "The only blanket my grandson has! You must get it back. Nykola will need it for the rest of the journey."

Dymtro pushed her hand off his arm.

"The sailors have blankets for sale," he said.

"We have no money to buy blankets," said Granny, shrilly.

People trying to sleep called out to them to be quiet. Nykola stared at Dymtro. Wasn't he a friend?

Granny saw that it was useless to expect help. She hobbled back to bed. "Here, Nykola, you must take my blanket," she said. "I will cover myself with my coat."

Next morning, as Nykola was climbing down past Josef's bunk, the man rolled over and his mattress shifted slightly. Underneath it was the stolen blanket.

Nykola gasped and almost cried out, but Josef, staring hard into Nykola's eyes, spoke first.

"What's wrong, my little son?"

Nykola just stared at Josef. How could he accuse the man of theft? No one would think it unusual for a father to use his son's blanket.

"Nothing's wrong," he muttered.

Josef grunted. "Get down. I want my breakfast."

Nykola slid past Ivan's empty bunk and scrambled under the table to Granny.

"Josef Koumka has my blanket," he whispered.

"Are you sure?"

"Yes, I saw it! What shall I do?"

"Oh, that Josef Koumka! That sly fellow! Why did the good Lord send him our way when we needed help?"

She sat up and glared across to where Josef was seated at the table.

He grinned.

"What's wrong, old woman?" he called. "Have you had a bad dream?"

Before Granny could answer, the sailors came in with the morning mush.

"We can do nothing, little one," said Granny. "Go, eat your breakfast."

As soon as Nykola had eaten, he hurried up on deck. He wanted his blanket back! There was no use asking Dymtro again, but surely Ivan would help him? Ivan would make two of little Josef. Ivan had only to roar and Josef would hand over the stolen property. Fortunately, the big man was standing alone beside the ship's railing. Nykola hurried over to him.

"Well, my early bird! And what news have you for me this beautiful morning?" he asked.

"Oh, Uncle," said the little boy, "my blanket was stolen!"

Ivan looked grave, but he spoke lightly.

"That is stale news, my birdie. You made enough noise about that last night. You and your Granny."

"But, Uncle, I know where it is!"

"Do you?"

Ivan stared calmly out at the black waves.

"Yes! Josef Koumka has it!"

"Ah, your father."

"You know he's not my father. He stole my blanket."

Ivan turned toward the hatch as a group of noisy children pushed through.

Nykola spoke urgently. "Get it back for me, Ivan. Please! Josef will give it to you."

The man would not meet Nykola's eyes. He merely shrugged and began to move toward the other children.

"Please, Ivan Tabaka!"

"What can I do?" asked Ivan, without

turning around. "I can do nothing." He spoke almost angrily. When Nykola didn't answer, he turned to look at him. "Come," he said, more gently, "come and dance with the other children."

Nykola looked at him with tear-filled eyes. Ivan wouldn't help him! Why was he such a coward? Surely he wasn't afraid of that lazy, little man? Why wouldn't he get back the blanket? Wasn't he Nykola's friend?

No, of course he wasn't. Nykola had been fooling himself. He and Granny had no friends.

CHAPTER 9

The New Land

From then on, the ship seemed to Nykola more and more like a prison. He longed to escape from the crowded, smelly hold, from Ivan, and especially from Josef Koumka. He sometimes wondered if he would ever see his family again. At last, one evening, Dymtro announced that the ship would be landing in Halifax the next day. Nykola could hardly believe it! All day, there had been nothing to look at but the same empty, grey sea. How did the sailors know they were near land?

"I knew it!" exclaimed Ivan. "I smelt the land when I was on deck just now."

"So did I!"

"And I."

"Me, also!"

Nykola wanted to rush up on deck and try to smell the land, too. But no one was allowed to leave the hold until after breakfast the next morning.

By then, there was no doubt that they were near land. All the steerage passengers went up on deck, even Granny. Nykola wriggled his way into a place at the ship's rail and gazed hungrily at the shoreline on the horizon. People were pointing to the land and drawing their families and friends up to the rail to show it to them. Through all the bustle, Nykola held his place. He was hardly aware of anyone else. He knew that his father's farm was nowhere near Halifax and that his family did not even know that he was coming. And yet, as he stood at the rail gazing at the land coming nearer and nearer, he felt sure that in a few minutes he would see the forest clearing that his father had described in his letter. There would be the little house, with his mother standing at the door. He and Granny would step off the ship and hurry into her arms.

This picture was so vivid in his mind that he could not believe they had arrived in Canada, even when he saw the docks and brick warehouses of the busy port of Halifax. It looked so much like Hamburg.

He turned to Granny, who was sitting on a coil of rope behind him.

"I don't see any farms," he said.

"No. We have a long way to go yet," she answered in a weary voice.

Since the theft of her grandson's blanket, she had been afraid to sleep in case Josef stole the rest of their money. Once they were on land, she thought, perhaps she could sleep.

Suddenly, the ship's whistle let out a long blast.

"We're going to dock!"

Many of the passengers, including Nykola, cheered loudly. It didn't matter how far they had yet to travel. Soon, soon, they would actually set foot in the new land!

There was a long, weary wait before that happened. When it did, the steerage passengers only moved to an immigration shed on the dock that was not so different from their quarters on the ship.

"You must sleep here tonight," explained Dymtro. "Tomorrow the officials will check your papers and put you on the train for the west."

It was now early evening and they had been given no dinner on the ship. They must find food. A canteen had been opened at one end of the shed. Granny gave Nykola some money and sent him off with Josef and Daria. She and Vera stayed with the baggage.

The cubicle they had been assigned had no front wall. Anyone walking along the large, open hall could look in at the two dozing women. Suddenly, Granny saw two figures in the opening. For a moment, she thought she was back in the Ukraine. Or was she dreaming? One of the figures was a priest! He was not dressed like her own beloved Father, but there was no doubt that he was a clergyman. Granny stared stupidly as Vera heaved herself to her feet and greeted the man. The sound of her voice woke Granny completely. She stumbled forward, fell on her knees, and grasped the priest's outstretched hand. Tears poured down her wrinkled cheeks. The man spoke soothingly, but she couldn't understand a word. She looked beseechingly at Dymtro.

"Father is blessing you," said the interpreter.

The old woman bowed her head. The priest spoke again.

"Father asks if there is anything he can

get for you. His parishioners wish to help you in your new life."

"A blanket?" asked Granny eagerly. "Could we have a blanket for my little grandson?"

The interpreter explained to the priest and he made a note in his black book. Before it was time to sleep, the blanket had been delivered.

"Oh," said Tetiana, "what a good land is this new land! One has only to ask for what one wants. And there is a church here, too. I heard the bells and I saw a priest! I was so afraid we had left the church behind."

She spread the new blanket on the floor for Nykola and lay down beside him.

"And the bed stays still again," she laughed. "Oh, we will be happy in this new land, Nykolenko."

Early next morning, Josef sidled up to Granny.

"Today," he said, "we must go before the officials who will let us enter Canada. You know that, don't you?"

"Yes," answered Granny suspiciously.

"They don't want old women and youngsters in this country. They'll send you two back on the ship."

"No, they won't!" cried Nykola. "They think we're part of your family."

Josef raised his eyebrows.

"My family?" he said. "No, no. You're no kin of mine."

"You told them we were!" Nykola said.

"You cheat! You thief!" Granny hissed. "What do you want now?"

"Well, now, what a way to talk to a man who has been a good friend to you." Josef turned away as if offended. "I'm glad you're not my relatives. Such ingratitude!"

"We won't be sent back," said Nykola. "We're going to my mother and father!"

Granny repeated, "What do you want, Josef Koumka?"

The peasant scratched his neck behind the ear.

"Well, now," he said, "back in Hamburg, did you promise me a gold coin if I told the officials you were my family? I think you did. I remember that I put you down as my mother and my son. But, I don't remember getting a coin. Perhaps you will give it to me now and I won't have to tell these officials that you don't belong to me."

"But I did pay you," wailed Tetiana. "We have only a few kopeks to buy food for the journey after we have paid for our train tickets. I cannot give you a gold coin."

"Well, now, I think you will have to find one, eh?" He nodded at Nykola. "Have you looked in the boy's coat lining, for instance?"

"But that coin will only just pay for the train tickets!" Granny's hands were clasped so tightly that the big white knuckles stood out like stones in a field. "Indeed, Josef Koumka, I have no other gold coin. I cannot give you what I haven't got."

"And I can't tell lies to get poor beggars into Canada," said Josef angrily. He walked away.

Nykola and Granny looked at one another with frightened eyes. What could they do?

"We must ask Ivan Tabaka for help, little Nykola," she said. "He is a big, strong peasant such as they want in this country. No one would refuse him entry. We will ask him to say we are his family."

But when they found Ivan in the throng, he refused them.

"I daren't tell lies to the officials, Granny," he said. "I don't want to answer too many questions. We're all so close to freedom in this new country. We don't want to be sent back, do we? If we tell lies, we might be found out." He could not meet the eyes of the boy who looked pleadingly up at him. He turned abruptly away. "I won't do it! Pay that scoundrel!"

"But we have no money," groaned Granny.

Ivan was gone. For a few minutes, the old lady and the boy stood still. Then the jostling of the crowd roused Nykola.

"Come, Granny," he said, taking her hand.

Dymtro Malkovitch stood near the door of the office waiting for the clerks to finish with the first group of people. Nykola pushed his way up to him. He told Dymtro how Josef had refused to take them into Canada as his family unless they gave him more money. By this time, Josef himself had come close and was listening. There was a hopeful grin on his face. Dymtro watched Josef while listening to Nykola.

At the end, he said, "Josef Koumka is right. Some people aren't wanted in Canada. Thieves, for example." Josef began to look uncomfortable. "But," went on Dymtro, "there's no trouble about entering if you have a family to go to."

Resting a paper against the wall, he wrote busily for a moment. Then he pinned a tag on Nykola's coat. One side said, 'DAUPHIN via WINNIPEG' and the other 'Nykola Ganczer, en route to his father, Wasyl Ganczer, farmer, Dauphin, Manitoba.' Granny's tag was similar. He motioned them through the door to the immigration officials.

"Your turn next," he said cheerfully.

Josef stared open-mouthed.

CHAPTER 10

Ivan Proves a Friend

That was the last they saw of Dymtro. They had been lucky that the ship's interpreter spoke their language. The immigration officer on the train did not speak Ukrainian. He was older than Dymtro; a tired, fussy man.

In Nykola's coach, most of the passengers were Ukrainian and the agent groaned when he saw the blank faces staring at him as he explained the arrangements. With the help of some German-speaking men, he finally made them understand that the journey would last three days. The train would stop two or three times a day. Those who wanted to could get out and buy food at the stations. There were stoves at each end of the coaches for those who had food with them. No one was to leave the train except to buy food.

When the train was underway, it was

much like the ship—overcrowded, stuffy, smelly, and the same constant motion. The difference, as the passengers were quick to see, was that the train stopped occasionally. It was possible to escape from the coach for a few minutes in the open air.

Ivan was the first man to try this. The second time the train stopped, Ivan stepped out and walked along beside the coach, grinning back at those inside. At the next stop, more passengers joined him and quite a crowd collected on the station platform. The agent scurried back from his coach up ahead and tried to shoo them all back inside. They pretended not to understand and stayed out until the whistle blew. Then there was a great scramble to get on board and much laughter.

Nykola watched all this wide-eyed. He would have gone out himself, but Granny held on to his arm.

"No, Nykola," she said. "What would I do if the train went on without you?"

Ivan puzzled Nykola. Once again, he was noisy and friendly, as he had been on the ship. But Nykola was wary. The big man had let him down twice. Why should he make friends again? But even so, he felt that Ivan was watching over them.

At night, Nykola slept with his coat for a pillow. During the day, he left it with his grandmother. But she dozed a lot and he worried that Josef might try to steal the coat during one of her naps.

One day, Nykola was visiting some children at the end of their coach. Granny, alone in her section, had fallen asleep with her head against the windowsill. Nykola's coat was safely tucked between her bundle and the back of the seat. Suddenly, he heard a tremendous fuss from the other end of the coach and hurried back to find Ivan had seized Josef by the wrists.

"Oh, ho! So, Josef Koumka! Once a thief, always a thief, eh?" he was saying. "What are you taking this time? The boy's coat? That is far too small for you, Josef! What is wrong with your eyes, my friend?"

Ivan shook Josef's arm till the coat dropped. Then he stood squarely in the way so that neither Vera nor her husband could escape. By this time, many other passengers were watching the scene.

"On the ship," continued Ivan, "you took my boots which were much too large. And now you want to steal this coat which is much too small." He was enjoying himself very much. "But, the blanket, now. I seem to remember a blanket. Is that right, Nykola?" He smiled at the bewildered boy. "Did this little man steal your blanket?"

Granny was awake now. "Yes, yes, he did!" she said. She snatched the coat from the floor and hugged it to her. "Thief! Thief!" she yelled at Josef.

Ivan reached over Vera, gripped Josef by the shoulders and lifted him out into the aisle. Several people laughed as Nykola ducked out of the way of Josef's flailing legs.

"Now, Josef Koumka," said Ivan, quietly and reasonably, "I think we will have that blanket back, if you please."

"I haven't got his blanket," said Josef sullenly.

Ivan tightened his grip. "I think you have," he said, still speaking pleasantly. He turned to his prisoner's wife. "Will you get the blanket, Vera Barsky, or shall I hold this little fellow upside down by the heels?"

"Let me go!" screamed Josef. "Let me go or I'll tell what I know about you, Ivan Tabaka!" Lowering his voice, he hissed, "Army deserter!"

Nykola stared with frightened eyes at Ivan. In his imagination, he saw Uncle Stefan being marched off by the soldiers back in the town square in Leleshen.

Ivan just laughed. "Yes, that's right. Deserter! But who cares?" He looked up and down the coach. "Do you think anyone here wants to go back to the Ukraine to tell the army about me?" Some of the men grinned. Ivan gave Josef a little shake. "Do you want to go back yourself and tell them? Well, Josef Koumka?"

"The officials here might like to know. Did you think of that?" Josef asked shrilly.

"Bah! What do they care? That's all behind me. I've got my papers now admitting me to Canada. Nobody is going to send me anywhere except to my brother's farm. Come, now. You have nothing on me! Hand over that blanket!"

He made a motion as if to up-end his victim.

Vera, frightened, called out to her daughter. "Daria, bring the blanket! Quickly! Quickly!"

"That's right, little mother," said Ivan approvingly. "You are much wiser than your husband."

Daria flung the blanket at Ivan. He took his hands off Josef to catch it.

Quickly, the would-be thief slunk off to his own section of the coach.

Ivan grinned at Nykola. "Well, my young sergeant, are you glad to have your blanket again?"

"Oh, yes! Thank you!"

Ivan sat down beside Granny and laid the blanket in her lap.

"Thank you, Ivan Tabaka," she said.

"I told you he had my blanket," said Nykola. "Why wouldn't you get it for me on the ship?"

"Because, my young friend, Josef guessed that I was a deserter from the Austrian army. If he had told the ship's officers or the immigration officials in Halifax, they might have sent me back. . . . Just might, mind you. But I wasn't going to take any chances. Now I'm in Canada and no one will bother to send me all the way back to the Ukraine." He laughed. "Just let them try! I'd be hard to find in all that bush, eh?" He waved his arm at the scene out the window.

Nykola laughed happily. It was good to have the big man for a friend again. Now Granny and Nykola were not afraid to get off the train whenever it made one of its brief halts. Ivan was always on hand to help the old woman on board. The agent had long ago given up trying to keep everyone on the train. For Granny and many others, the stops prevented the motion sickness they had suffered on the ship.

The long, three days' journey was slowly coming to an end. A train official began to organize the passengers into different groups. All those wearing Dauphin tags were gathered in one coach. It was time for goodbyes.

Ivan Tabaka, who was going on to Edmonton, was not allowed to enter the Dauphin coach. He stood with them at the door, steadying Granny as the train swayed.

"Goodbye, my young friend," he said cheerfully. "I almost wish I could be with you when you surprise your family, but I'll be busy surprising my own." He laughed and rumpled Nykola's hair. To Tetiana, he said, "God be with you, Granny. May you live many years in comfort in the home of your daughter."

"If only the good Lord lets me live to see my grandson reunited with his mother and father, I shall die in peace," she answered.

"No, no! You will live many more years. I feel it! Goodbye, now. God be with you both."

CHAPTER 11
Dauphin

Nykola felt very much alone now that Ivan had gone. But he had done them one great favour. Josef Koumka left them strictly alone. After the train arrived in Winnipeg, they never saw Josef and his family again. Josef decided to stay in the city with his wife and daughter and look for work there.

At Winnipeg, the Dauphin group were marched into yet another immigration shed. Once again, they lined up in front of a desk. Ever since they had fled from the Ukraine, Granny and Nykola had been surrounded by crowds of strangers and ordered about by officials, most of whom they could not understand.

The weather was terribly hot. The temperature in the streets was ninety degrees. In the crowded shed, it must have been over a hundred. None of the people in the line-up had had a chance to bathe or wash their clothes for over two weeks. Nykola took very shallow breaths and watched Granny anxiously. Was she going to faint?

Now, here was another man in uniform. After looking at their papers, the officer sent them to a desk where they had to buy train tickets. The clerk had a hard time making Granny understand that they must pay out more money.

"We have only a few kopeks left," she said. "We can't give them up!"

Finally, Nykola took the money from her and paid. Holding her elbow, he steered her into a waiting room and led her to a bench. Granny sank down gratefully.

Listening to the excited chatter around them, Nykola learned that the Dauphin train was waiting and they would be put aboard soon. They would sleep on the train and be in Dauphin next morning.

Dauphin! Nykola's eyes shone. He forgot about being tired, hot, and worried. He turned to Granny.

"Did you hear?" he asked.

"Yes, Nykolenko. Soon we'll be there," she whispered. Her eyes, too, brightened with happiness.

After a restless night on the train, Nykola woke very early the next morning. Eagerly, he looked out the window to see bush on both sides of the track. This looked like the country his father had described in the letter that Uncle Stefan had read so long ago back home. They must be getting close to Dauphin.

The coach was almost empty. Most of the other travellers had left the train yesterday at stations on the flat, open plains. Two other family groups and he and Granny were the only ones left. As he looked around, Isydora Jatsin, a young mother of three, spoke to him in a low voice while a baby slept in her lap.

"Well, young Nykola, this is a great day for us all, eh? The end of our long journey! I can tell you, I'll be glad to see my brother-in-law! I hope he received the telegram."

Nykola's glow of excitement was dampened by doubt.

"Telegram?" he asked.

"Yes, we sent a telegram from one of those little stations before we reached Winnipeg. I should say one of the officials did it for us. So that he would meet this train. Didn't you? To your father, I mean?"

Before Nykola could answer, one of her other children woke and she turned to attend to him.

"What was she saying, Nykola?" asked Granny in a sleepy voice.

Nykola turned an anxious face to the old lady.

"Granny, Father doesn't know to meet us. How will we get to his farm?"

Granny looked blankly back at him.

"I don't know." She frowned. "I guess we made a mistake. We should have asked someone how to let Wasyl Ganczer know we were coming."

"Yes," answered her grandson, in a worried voice.

He glanced out the window. Many of the leaves on the trees were already turning yellow or brown. Some had fallen. The bush did not look very welcoming. Where in all this wilderness was his father's farm?

Granny stood up and shook her skirt into place. She smiled at the boy.

"Don't look so worried, Nykolenko. We are almost at Dauphin! If the good Lord brought us so far, he will show us the way to your father. Have faith! Soon, soon we will see your mother again."

Nykola did have faith in Granny. He

returned her smile. Nothing could spoil for long the excitement of arriving at last in Dauphin. As the train slowed down, he rushed to a window and pressed his face against it. The coach cleared the bush and he had a glimpse of wooden buildings, a dirt road with three ox-drawn wagons, and then a dull, red station house with a sign reading DAUPHIN. They had arrived!

Isydora's husband, Luka Jatsin, leaned over Nykola to stare out the window. Suddenly, he gave a great shout and ran to the door. Almost before the train had stopped, he leapt to the platform and Nykola watched as two brothers embraced and slapped one another on the back.

Out on the platform, Nykola and Granny felt very lonely as they stood among the others who were all being greeted by relatives. At last, the young, bearded immigration agent noticed them. He looked at a paper. "You must be Tetiana Doroshenko and Nykola Ganczer."

"Yes," answered Granny.

"No one has come to meet you, yet?"

"No," said Granny.

"My father doesn't know we are here," said Nykola.

"And who is your father?"

"Wasyl Ganczer."

"Ah, I know him. He came a year ago and took a homestead to the north. Is that him?" Nykola nodded. He looked at the two anxious faces and suddenly smiled. "It's nothing to worry about. We'll take care of you. Look, right now I must see to all these people. Do you see that big tent?"

They looked where he pointed, at the huge tent that stood in an empty field between the station and the main road of the town. They nodded again.

"You can wait there. There are beds and stoves. Go and make yourselves comfortable till I have time, then I will see to you."

The tent had been set up to accommodate dozens of people. It seemed cold and lonely with only the two of them in it. Nykola and Granny placed their bundles on the nearest cots and went back to where Luka and his brother were loading a wagon with baggage and children. While they worked, the other two wagons left.

When the Jatsins were ready, the agent ticked off their names from his list.

"Have a good journey," he said.

"Wait! Wait!" called Isydora from the front seat she was sharing with her old mother. "What about our friends here?

How will they reach Nykola's father? Can we take them?"

"Take them, woman! Where would we put them?" demanded her brother-in-law. "There's no room. Besides, Ganczer's place is in the other direction from mine. It would take an extra day to deliver them."

"What you *can* do," said the agent, "is to send word to Ganczer. Will you? Stop at Sawchuk's place at the crossroads and ask them to pass on the message."

"Yes. Gladly will I do that. Cheer up, youngster," he said to Nykola, who had listened to all this with a long face. "Your father will soon hear that you are waiting for him."

He prodded the ox and the heavily-laden wagon moved off with the two men and the older boy walking alongside. Nykola watched with a sinking heart. When would his father come?

The agent showed Nykola the wood-pile and the axe. He handed him the water pail and pointed out the pump. To Granny, he gave a sack of vegetables and a small loaf of bread. Then he left them, saying he had a lot of paperwork to do. Preparing and eating a meal took up very little time. The long, empty afternoon and evening hours stretched ahead. Granny lay down for a nap, but Nykola was too restless to sleep. He decided to explore this town which had been their goal for so long.

In the early afternoon, the little town was quiet. Across the street from the tent was a large, three-storey building with a flag flying from the roof. Nykola saw a girl come out of the side door and throw dish-water on the garden. There was no other sign of life. To the left there were two streets of wooden houses, just as quiet. Nykola decided to walk the other way where a wide road crossed the railway tracks and disappeared from his view to the right of a hotel. He crossed the field, stepped up onto the wooden sidewalk and walked slowly down the street. There were shops and businesses on each side; a few men and women entered or left them. A farm wagon, drawn by a scrawny, brown ox and heavily loaded with fire-wood, passed by on the dusty roadway.

Where the next street crossed, Nykola saw a small building flying a flag like the one on the hotel. As he paused at the corner, two little girls came skipping out of the building onto the sidewalk. Catch-ing sight of the strange boy, they stopped and stared. Then they began to giggle. They joined hands and ran off down the street, peeking over their shoulders and giggling again.

Nykola was still wondering what the girls found so funny about him, when three boys, after jostling each other in the doorway, tumbled out onto the weedy schoolyard. They, too, stopped and stared at Nykola. One said something and the other two laughed. They began to walk toward him. Although he didn't understand their language, he knew they were unfriendly. He began to walk backwards. After a few steps, he began to fear that he might trip and he did not want to fall in front of them. He turned around. He was not going to show that he was afraid by running, but he did walk quickly down the empty street. The boys stayed close behind, calling names at him all the time. Just as Nykola passed the door of the harness shop, a clod of mud hit him in the back and a man stepped out of the store. The man roared. Nykola, not sure who the man was yelling at, broke into a run and raced back to the shelter of the tent. Nobody followed him.

From then on, Nykola stayed away from the town. The agent showed him which road his father would use to come into town.

"But he can't possibly get here tomorrow, you know. He might not get the message for several days. It depends on whether anyone is going that way."

Nevertheless, Nykola spent the whole of the next day, except for mealtimes, sitting at the side of the road. It seemed to make him closer to his family and, out there, he was out of sight of the hateful town.

On the third day, Nykola left the tent early in the morning to find a light frost covering the ground. And yet, the afternoon before, he had been so hot that he had fallen asleep at his post. Now, he went inside to get his boots. As he pulled them on, he heard voices nearby.

One was saying, "Stefan Ganczer? No. There's a young boy, Nykola Ganczer. Would that be him?"

"He's here!" gasped Nykola.

Granny's hands flew to her face.

Nykola raced outside and stopped short. Just a few feet away stood two men; the immigration agent and his father!

CHAPTER 12

Family Reunion

Suddenly, Nykola was shy. "Batechko? Father?" he called timidly.

Wasyl Ganczer whirled around. Nykola stared at the man who was almost a stranger to him. He looked just the same; tall and strong. His black hair was still shaggy and rumpled. He was clean-shaven but still had the black, full eyebrows that could draw together to make him look so fierce when he was angry. Would his father be glad to see him? That question was answered when Wasyl swept him up in a bear hug that lifted his feet off the ground.

"My son! My son!" said Wasyl. "You're really here!"

He set Nykola down and, still holding him, examined him in delight. "Nykola, my son, and what a fine, big son you'll be! But, tell me," he went on, looking all around, "where is Stefan Ganczer? Where is my brother? How did he get out of the army? The last we heard, you weren't coming at all and then yesterday a neighbour stops by and says my son is at the railway station in Dauphin. What rejoicing! Your mother cried buckets. How did it happen? Tell me all about it."

Nykola laughed up at his father. "Granny brought me," he said triumphantly, pointing to the tent where the old lady stood grinning in the doorway.

"Tetiana Doroshenko! You here?" exclaimed Wasyl. "But I don't understand. How is this? Where's Stefan?"

His surprise and bewilderment delighted Nykola.

"Uncle Stefan couldn't bring me! He's in the army. So, Granny brought me."

"What? You two? I can hardly believe it! Did you two come all by yourselves on that long journey?"

"Yes, yes," cried Nykola excitedly, as Granny nodded and smiled.

Wasyl shook his head. "Well," he said two or three times. Suddenly, he shrugged off his bewilderment.

"Come," he said. "You can tell me all about it as we go home. Give me your baggage. The wagon is on the road."

Before long, Nykola and Granny found themselves sitting in a farm wagon much like the one that had taken them away from Uncle Feodor's farm. Only three weeks ago! With what different feelings Nykola looked up the road past the ox, Bess. Then he had been frightened; now he felt safe. Then he had been sad; now he felt happy. And as he and Granny told their story to Wasyl, who exclaimed with horror, or pity, or admiration at the right times, he began to feel courageous. It was a great thing that they had done, to come so far and arrive safely.

Nykola's shyness had completely worn off long before they had travelled through the many miles of bush to his father's clearing. Wasyl was full of enthusiasm for this new land. He talked at length of all that he had already done and meant to do on his homestead. Just beyond the town, a prairie fire had swept through only the week before, burning out many new settlers. But even the black, desolate ruin they passed did not depress him.

"They'll start again," he said. "That's one of the wonders of this new land. You can start again."

As they rode along, he pointed out

homesteads belonging to other Ukrainians and seemed to take great pride in them all. The closer they came to his own land, the more excited he became. He sat up straighter and talked louder. Unfortunately, the farther they went from Dauphin, the worse the road became, until now it was a mere track through the bush. The ox went slower and slower as the footing became rougher. The wagon bounced and jolted horribly. Wasyl and Nykola jumped down and walked beside Bess. Granny stayed in the wagon. She no longer talked or listened, but seemed only to be trying to endure the fearful ride. At last, the wagon stopped. Nykola came to her side.

"Granny," he said, "are you coming?"

She looked at him dazedly. "What is it, Nykola?"

He pointed ahead. In the doorway of a rough cabin stood a woman with a baby in her arms. On either side, a child pressed so close to her that it was hard to see anything of them.

"Marfa! Marfa!" murmured the old woman.

With tears dimming her eyes, she climbed quickly over the wheel and hobbled toward the group. Nykola followed

close behind. Once again, he was shy. He had never seen this baby. And the two little girls—were they really the little girls he remembered?

As he stared, one child stepped away from her mother's side and smiled shyly. He smiled back. Larysa! She was taller, but her long, brown braids were the same and so was her round face and the grave expression in her eyes. Baby Olaha was a baby no longer. She had grown even more than Larysa, and her hair was pulled into two stubby braids. Keeping her eyes averted from the newcomers, she ran quickly to her father and watched them from the safety of his arms.

Meanwhile, Granny had taken the baby in her arms and was crooning over it. Nykola's mother was hugging him, wetting his cheeks with her tears. She was just the same—short and plump, with the same round face the two girls had and dark, braided hair. Nykola remembered that her expression had usually been worried but now her face was bright with joy.

"Come in," she said. "Come in to your home!"

Although Marfa had prepared a feast (from rabbits the girls had snared, cabbage grown in their own garden, and fresh bread), they were all too excited to pay much attention to what they were eating. They all exclaimed how wonderful it was that the two had accomplished the terrible journey all by themselves. Marfa described how she and the girls had lived in the cold, drafty tent with many other families for weeks while the men selected homesteads and built rude shelters. They were glad that Granny and Nykola had been spared that.

The house had only one room, but Marfa and Wasyl had built it well. First, they had made walls with poplar logs, and roof rafters with smaller logs. Then the walls, both inside and out, were plastered thickly with a mixture of clay, water, and chopped straw. Larysa, and even little Olaha, had helped with that. Olaha had often been plastered as thick as the wall at the end of a day.

Inside the house, the big stove was made in the same way. As at home in the Ukraine, the flat top of the stove served as a bed for the children. A framework of poplar logs in a corner made a bed for the parents. Benches and tables were also homemade, but Wasyl had bought two windows and a door in Dauphin at the same time he had bought the ox. The tall grass that grew on the low parts of their land made an excellent thatch for the roof.

When the house was finished, they had moved in and left the first crude building as a shelter for Bess. Marfa had brought some of her kilims[8] with her from the old country and two of these woven hangings now hung from long poles near the ceiling. They provided a splash of bright colour against the grey, mud walls at each end of the room. Someday, Marfa thought, she would have both whitewash and paint to brighten up their home. Meanwhile, she was overjoyed to have her family united once more.

Later, when the three children were in bed, but not yet asleep, Granny, cuddling the baby, looked around happily. Wasyl had kicked off his boots and was lying propped up on the bed, resting. His wife was busy mending a tear in Nykola's shirt. The candle by which she worked was the only light in the room. It was dusk, but a little light came in through the open door and uncurtained windows.

"God has been good to you," said Granny.

Wasyl grunted contentedly.

"It's a fine country," he said. "We have

[8]kē'lēm a woven tapestry or carpet.

done well and will do better now that I have my son to help me."

Nykola grinned happily in the semi-darkness. Here he was wanted and loved; not like at his uncle's house.

"I must thank you, Tetiana Doroshenko," said Wasyl gravely and formally, "for bringing my son to me."

Granny replied in the same formal manner.

"With God's help, I did what had to be done. I'm glad you are pleased, Wasyl Ganczer."

After a moment's silence, she turned to her daughter.

"It was the good Lord who brought your son safely to this farm, my daughter. You and I must go together to the church to offer thanks. When can we go?"

It was Wasyl who answered. "There's no church here!" he said harshly.

"Ah, so I feared! So I feared!" said Granny. "But we can see the priest. When will he come?"

"There are no priests in the new land!" Wasyl said.

His wife looked distressed and whispered, "Hush."

"But I saw one when we landed off the ship," Granny said. "He gave us a blanket. Yes, there are priests in the new land."

Wasyl swung his legs off the bed, leaned forward, and pointed his finger at the old woman.

"Well, there are none here and never will be, I hope! We get on very well without interfering priests!"

In his bed, Nykola winced. His stomach knotted. He pulled the blanket over his head, making a peephole with his hand. Were his father and grandmother going to quarrel on the very first day?

Granny said no more. She knew there were priests in the new land and she was determined to find one.

CHAPTER 13

The Peddler

For Granny there was no church and for Nykola and his sisters, no school. They spent their time working on the farm. Every morning, Nykola and Larysa went out with pick and hoe to dig up roots and large stones. Little Olaha followed to pick up any small stones the others left behind.

Sometimes Marfa sighed over the life her children led. "They should be in school," she said, "not slaving on the land."

"Someday, there'll be a school," answered her husband. "You'll see! All the land between here and the crossroads will be taken up and there'll be plenty of children. Then we'll have a school!"

"But when?" asked Marfa, plopping wearily onto a chair for a few minutes' rest. "At home in the Ukraine there was at least a school for them to go to. And we're just as poor here as we were there, too."

"Not so!" declared Wasyl. "In one year's time this land will be mine! All 160 acres of it! My own! Sure, it's hard work now, but you'll see, in a few years we'll have a good farm here."

"And when I'm sixteen, I can file for my own homestead," put in Nykola. "Why in ten years we'll be as rich as lords!"

His mother smiled. "Well, maybe."

"Try counting your blessings, wife," boomed Wasyl. "Haven't we plenty to eat—rabbit meat and good vegetables? Haven't we all the wood and water we need?"

Marfa grimaced at that. She had spent most of the day helping to cut down trees to clear more land. Staring at her calloused hands, she replied, "Yes, yes, I do not mean to complain."

"If only it weren't so lonely here," Granny sighed. "I miss the village."

"You have your daughter and the children," Wasyl said impatiently.

"Ah, it's fine for you to talk," said his wife. "It's not hard for you to walk almost a mile to the only neighbour's place. And in the winter, you go to work with the gang and see other people. I know what

Granny means. It is lonely for us women—stuck out in the bush with only ourselves for company."

The days passed and it was almost November. Winter had begun. Wasyl began to talk of leaving them for a few weeks to work again for the contractor who was cutting ties for the railway, which was to be built from Dauphin to Wolf River. With Nykola's help, he cut a huge supply of wood. For meat, he killed a deer. The children would be able to snare rabbits. He was waiting now for word to come that the logging had begun.

Because of the cold weather, Nykola was now indoors much more. He noticed how frail and slow Granny had become. One morning, she could not get up at all. Nykola left his place at the breakfast table to take a glass of hot tea to her. He supported her while she sipped it.

"What's wrong, Granny?" he asked in a frightened whisper.

"Such a pain I have, my little Nykola!" Her voice was weak and quavery. "Thank you for the tea. Let me lie down now."

Marfa frowned as she looked over at her.

"What can I do for you, Mother?" she asked.

"Nothing. Nothing. I'm dying, I think."

"No, no!" boomed Wasyl, turning right round on the bench to smile at her. "What nonsense! Why would you die? A little indigestion perhaps."

"But she hasn't eaten anything for two days," protested his wife.

"Ha!" he said, triumphantly. "Weak! That's what it is! Come, Granny, you must eat and get well. We can't spare you yet. Larysa, take her a crust to dip in the tea."

He broke a piece off the loaf that stood in the centre of the table.

"No, I thank you, Wasyl. I can eat nothing."

She waved Larysa away.

Nykola knelt on the dirt floor beside the bed.

"What can we do for you, Granny?" he asked.

"Get me a priest, Nykola," she answered, quietly.

But Wasyl heard her.

"No priest!" he said. "There's no priest here. I told you that already."

Granny raised her head.

"There must be a priest somewhere. You could find him when you go to the logging, Wasyl. Find the priest and send him to me, I beg you."

Wasyl turned red. He pushed back the bench roughly and stamped toward the door.

"No priest!" he said again. "No priest shall set foot in my house!"

He strode out into the yard.

No one spoke for a moment. Granny sighed and turned her face to the wall where her icon hung. Nykola looked pleadingly at his mother, but she would not meet his eyes. Instead, she spoke harshly to the little girls, telling them to hurry with their breakfast.

Later, when Nykola came in to supper with his father, he was glad to see Granny sitting at the table holding the baby. Nobody said anything about her illness. As soon as they were all seated, they heard a shout in the yard. This was so unusual that for a few seconds no one moved.

Then Wasyl opened the door. Coming toward the house they saw a little man with a big pack on his back. A wide, friendly grin split his face above a black, scraggly beard. He wore a red woollen tuque, a long black overcoat, heavy sailors' trousers, and Indian moccasins. As he came closer, he pulled off darned, woollen mittens and thrust them deep into his huge pockets. Shy Olaha jumped up and ran to the door.

"The peddler! The peddler!" she cried.

In the spring, he had given her a little china dog for her very own. It was the only toy she had ever had that was hers alone. She thought the peddler was the most wonderful person in the world.

"Welcome! Welcome!" said Wasyl, as the peddler came in and slipped off his pack.

"Just in time for supper," said Marfa, with a big smile. "Welcome. Come and sit down."

The peddler pulled off his tuque and greeted everybody.

"Peace be on this house," he said, bowing to each in turn. "Ah, ha! Here are Tetiana Doroshenko and Nykola Ganczer. I have been hearing about these two world travellers."

Nykola laughed. The peddler spoke Ukrainian with such a funny accent. And he made such comical faces! His wink at Nykola was so elaborate that the whole side of his face screwed up and the skin on his bald head wrinkled. He could also waggle his beard, and this he did to Daniel, who laughed up at him from Granny's lap.

The peddler intended to spend the night so there was time to linger over supper and listen to the news that he brought. First, he gave Wasyl a message from the contractor. Work had started and Wasyl should come as soon as possible. Their neighbour was ready with his ox and wagon whenever Wasyl should come with his beast.

"I'll travel with you tomorrow," said Wasyl.

"Good, good!" answered the peddler. "Who knows, we may fall in with the priest."

Granny looked up eagerly but Wasyl spoke first.

"What priest?" he demanded.

"Is there a priest coming?" Marfa asked. "We heard that the people in town were trying to get one."

"Yes, yes, but such doings!" said the peddler. "In Wolf River they told me that there are many babies to baptize and three couples to wed. All these waiting for the priest." He looked at Granny kindly. "And many old ones, eh, auntie, who want to see the holy man? Yes, yes, the storekeeper, Martin Staranchuk, he was in Dauphin to do business. He heard that a priest of your faith was travelling through the country and coming as far north as Dauphin. So he wrote to the holy man and begged him to come to Wolf River."

Marfa smiled. "Martin Staranchuk's daughter is one who wants to marry," she said.

Granny sat up. She stretched her hands toward her son-in-law.

"Oh, Wasyl Ganczer, could you find this priest and bring him to me?"

Wasyl scowled.

"No priest shall set foot in my house!"

"But my son," said Granny, "for a dying woman!"

"You're not dying," Wasyl answered.

Marfa spoke quietly. "No, indeed, Mother, you're not dying. Soon you'll be yourself again."

"If the good Lord wills it so," answered Granny. She crept over to her bed and lay down. "But I fear He does not. I want to see the priest and make my confession before I go."

"No priest!" shouted Wasyl.

Tears trickled down the old woman's cheeks but she made no sound. Larysa and Olaha slipped up onto the top of the stove. Nykola stared down at the floor. Although he felt sorry for Granny, he did not dare to speak.

During the quarrel, the peddler's eyes darted from the old lady to his host. In the uneasy silence, he said, "Well, there's more news to tell. Who do you think has a puppy with him today?"

"Is it you?" whispered Olaha. "Is it you, peddler?"

"Yes! Yes, it's me!"

"Where is it?" asked Larysa.

"Now, where did I put it?"

The peddler lifted his arms wide so that his shoulders touched his ears. He glanced down at his right-hand pocket and then at the left.

"Not here," he said, pretending to be puzzled.

Olaha giggled. "Is it in your pack?" she asked.

Nykola walked over to the corner and felt all over the bundle.

"No," he said. He was half-sure that the peddler was only teasing—that he had no puppy. But, if he had, where would it be? "I know," he shouted. "You left it out in the stable with Bess."

The man threw up his hands in astonishment.

"A genius as well as a world traveller! I remember now! That's just where I left him." He turned to Marfa. "May I bring him in and show the children, Mother?"

"Yes," Marfa answered. "You'll have to do that now. Look at them! They're sick with excitement."

"I'll get him," said Nykola.

The peddler nodded and Nykola hurried out.

"I'll just clear these dishes while you show the puppy," said Marfa, "and then we can look at your pack."

"Are you going to keep the pup?" asked Wasyl. He spoke in a normal tone, but his eyes were still dark with anger.

The man shrugged. "I was going to. I took him in trade for a length of dress goods. I thought he'd be company. But he's too young yet to walk the long distances I must walk and he's too heavy to carry."

Nykola came in carrying the dog. The two girls ran to him.

"Let me see!"

"Let me hold him!"

Wasyl laughed as the puppy licked each of the children in turn.

"Black as soot, he is!" he said.

"Sooty, Sooty," crooned Olaha.

She turned pleading eyes to her father. He understood. He motioned her to bring him the dog and examined him carefully. A farm needs a good dog, he thought.

"Will you sell him?" he asked.

Olaha squealed. Nykola and Larysa exchanged quick grins.

"What do you offer?" asked the peddler.

"The wife has some rabbit-skin hats like you took last time, eh, Marfa?"

His wife nodded. Smiling at the children, she came back to the table and sat down in front of the pack that the peddler had opened.

"I need sewing needles," she said. "And thread."

So the evening passed in bargaining, and nothing more was said about the priest.

Early in the morning, Wasyl and the peddler set off together. Wasyl would be gone a few weeks; the peddler would return in the spring. When he bent over Granny to say goodbye, he murmured, "The priest should be passing on the Dauphin road in two days' time, auntie."

The first day without their father passed slowly. Nykola woke in the night. Something was wrong. He could hear groans and a soothing voice. He raised his head and peered through the darkness to Granny's corner. His mother was bending over the old woman. Granny's groans reminded him of the night in Hamburg when he had awakened to find her ill and in pain. As he lay listening, he thought of all she had done for him. He knew that she would never have left her beloved Ukraine, if it hadn't been for him. The ocean voyage and the train had both made her sick. Yet she had struggled through it all and brought him to his family. Why wouldn't Father send the priest to her? He was cruel! Just because he hated priests!

The next day, Nykola took a turn sitting at Granny's bedside. Sometimes, he gave her a sip of water or wiped her fevered forehead. There was nothing else any of them could do for her.

Once she opened her eyes and saw him gazing at her.

"Nykola, my little Nykola," she whispered hoarsely, "do something for me."

"Anything, Granny! What is it? What can I do?"

"Go and get the priest, Nykola."

She seized his hand and held it fast.

"But, Granny...Father...Father said no...."

"Nykola! Little quail! I'm dying, my little one. Please! I cannot die without a

priest. Think, Nykola, of all the sins I have committed." Her voice became so weak that Nykola had to bend over to hear her. "And all for you, Nykola. I stole money. I lied. I have not made confession since I left my home." She groaned. "Oh, I am afraid to die until I have confessed."

Nykola tried to pull his hand away but her grip was too strong. What was he to do? His father would be very angry if he brought a priest into the house. And, anyway, how could he find the priest? And how persuade him to come if he did find him?

"Please, Nykola, get me the priest."

Her eyes stared unblinking into his. Was she really dying? The skin on the back of his neck prickled. His mouth felt dry.

"Granny, I don't know where the priest is," he said desperately.

She drew him closer. Her breath felt warm on his cheek.

Eagerly, she whispered, "The peddler told me. The priest will be on the road to town tomorrow. You could go to meet him and bring him here."

"But, Granny, he wouldn't come. How could I make him come?"

"Listen, Nykola!" She had used too much of her strength. Her voice was very weak and her hand fell from his arm. He bent closer still. "Nykola, behind the icon. . . ." She raised her eyes to the picture of St. Elizabeth. "Lift down the icon."

He looked around for help. There was no one else in the house except the baby asleep in his cradle. He lifted down the icon. Through the years, the picture had darkened and the colours had faded, but the saint's eyes remained bright and clear. They seemed to look directly into Nykola's eyes.

Granny raised her hand feebly.

"Look behind the picture. There is a coin. The last florin. Do you see it? Under the paper. . .there! There, you have it!" She sighed at the puzzled look on his face. "Yes, I lied about that, too. Nykola, take the coin to the priest. Tell him it's for the church. He will come." She closed her eyes. "And if he's too late, the florin will buy candles for my soul."

Nykola gripped the coin so tightly that the edge of it hurt his hand.

"Oh, no, Granny," he said.

Once again, she opened her eyes. With trembling hands she took the icon and held it against her heart.

"Nykola, go for the priest! Please!"

"Yes, Granny. I'll go!"

CHAPTER 14

A Scary Night

When he told his mother about going for the priest, she looked at him doubtfully.

"Your father will be angry," she said. "And yet..." She glanced at her mother. "Yes," she said, "you should go. But how will you find him?"

Nykola told her that the priest would be passing on the Dauphin road the next day.

"Tomorrow!" his mother exclaimed. "Then you can't fetch him! You can't go so far before tomorrow!"

They talked it over, keeping their voices low so as not to disturb Granny. The girls listened wide eyed.

"Is Nykola going alone?" asked Olaha. "Oh, I'd be scared."

"Hush!" said Marfa impatiently. "We're trying to decide what's best to do."

Martin Staranchuk would doubtless be driving the priest in his wagon. They would leave Dauphin early in the morning in order to be in Wolf River in good time. Would they stop to visit farmers on the way? There was no way of knowing exactly when they would pass the crossroads.

"I'll be there early in the morning," said Nykola. "Then I won't miss them."

"But, that means you'll have to start now," objected his mother.

"Yes."

Olaha began to cry. "He'll be out all night! The bears will get him!"

"Hush, you'll wake Granny," said Larysa.

Marfa looked troubled.

"No, Son," she said, "you can't be out all night. You would freeze. You must stay at the Englishman's place. You know where that is, don't you?"

"Yes, I know where it is," he answered. "But, Mother, I don't know him. I can't even speak to him."

"Do you want to stay home, Son? You don't have to go. Granny may be better soon."

Just then Tetiana groaned and her daughter hurried to her.

"Marfa, Marfa, please," begged the old lady. "Let Nykola go for the priest."

"Yes, yes, Little Mother, he is just going. Calm yourself."

"I'll leave right now," said Nykola.

With a worried frown, Marfa made up a bed roll and packed a lunch in a lard pail. When all was ready, Nykola pulled on his boots and sheepskin coat. He slung the bed roll round his shoulders, put on his rabbit-skin hat and mittens, and picked up the lard pail.

"I'm going, Granny," he called softly.

"God go with you," she answered.

When he opened the door, the dog came bounding out of the stable.

From behind him, Olaha shouted, "Take Sooty with you. He'll fight the bears!"

"That's a good idea," said her mother. "He's very small but maybe the dog smell will keep off the wild animals. Anyway, he'll be company."

"Yes," said Nykola with relief. "I'll take the pup."

At first, Sooty was delighted to be going for a walk. He raced back and forth across the road, running a little way into the bush on either side and barking excitedly at all the smells. But after an hour, he settled down to a steady pace, walking in the wagon rut parallel to Nykola's. The sun had gone behind the clouds and soon would be going down for the night. The woods were darker and more frightening. The boy knew he was still a long way from the Englishman's shack. Would he dare to walk through the bush in the dark?

He could go back, he thought. If he hurried, he could be back before it was pitch dark. At least he would be travelling on a familiar road rather than going to a stranger's place. He could tell Granny that the priest had already passed by. No! That wouldn't be right! He had promised Granny that he would bring the priest.

The puppy began to whimper and lag behind. Several times Nykola had to call him to hurry up.

At last, they reached the turnoff to the Englishman's shack. Although there was still enough light to see the beginning of the path, the woods behind looked black and forbidding. Nykola and Sooty hesitated for some minutes. Taking a deep breath, Nykola moved forward, calling the dog to follow him. They crossed a short stretch of long grass and thistles, making the dry stalks rustle as they passed through. As soon as they stepped into the bush, Sooty began to cringe and whimper.

"What is it, Sooty?" asked Nykola in a frightened whisper. "What's wrong?"

He bent to touch the dog, now pressed against his leg. Sooty's fur felt coarse and bristly under his hand. The hair on the boy's arm and on the back of his neck rose in the same way. But Nykola could see or hear nothing. He stood up. They couldn't stay here! It would be better to be moving. Back to the road or forward? Forward, of course. At least there was shelter ahead, even if the owner was a stranger.

Stiff-legged, Nykola walked down the narrow trail. The rustling of the branches he brushed, and the snapping of twigs underfoot, prevented him from hearing other sounds that he was sure were there in the dark. Yet, whenever he stopped to listen, he could hear nothing except the beating of his own heart.

Sooty, no longer whimpering, stayed close to the boy. After what seemed like a very long time, they came to a clearing with a house in the middle of it. Like his own house, it was made of logs, but instead of being completely plastered with mud, only the chinks had been filled. It was not a Ukrainian building.

Nykola's relief at getting safely through the bush turned to terrible shyness. How could he approach a stranger? The Englishman wouldn't understand him.

Should he shout from here? Or go and knock on the closed door? No light shone through the window. No smoke was rising from the chimney. The place looked deserted. Fear returned. In spite of the cold, he was sweating in his sheepskin coat. His stomach had shrunk to a hard knot, his mouth was dry, his eyes wide open. Sooty growled his puppy growl and gave a soft, tentative bark as if to ask what was wrong.

Nykola stared at the house. Deserted and cold, surrounded by the black bush, it looked sinister. Was it really the Englishman's shack or had he come upon the hut of the witch, Baba Yoga? The place was perfect for a witch. Could this be her house? Would she be coming back to it? He strained his ears to listen.

From old folk tales, he knew that Baba Yoga travelled in an iron mortar, which she pushed with an iron pestle. She was followed by a magic broom which swept away all traces of her passage so no one could follow her tracks. But she could be heard. Was she coming through the woods now? He listened with all his might, but he could hear nothing through the pounding of the blood in his ears.

Sooty, however, had had enough of the cold. Here was a man's house and warmth. Why not go in? He ran forward and pawed at the door. The movement woke Nykola from his terror. He shivered. It was very cold. He would have to go into the shack, he thought. It was, after all, just the Englishman's house. He knocked twice without conviction. Obviously, nobody was home. He pushed the door and it opened slowly with a creaking sound. Inside, it was pitch black.

When his eyes became used to the darkness, Nykola saw the stove. He found that it was laid, ready to be lit. A box of matches hung nearby. Should he light the stove? He would freeze if he didn't. He would re-lay the fire in the morning, he decided, and leave everything just as he had found it.

As he worked, he wondered whether the owner were coming back tonight. Would he be angry if he did come and found Nykola making himself at home? More likely he would be glad to enter a warm cabin. Nykola looked around. The room had a deserted air, as if nobody was living there just now. Perhaps he had gone to work on the railway as Wasyl had.

Meanwhile, Sooty ran around and sniffed at everything. He came back to the boy and looked up at him beseechingly. Wasn't it time to eat? he seemed to be saying. Nykola grinned at the little dog and gave him a pat.

"I'm hungry," he said. "Let's eat."

After they had shared half the lunch Marfa had packed, Sooty curled up under the stove and fell asleep. Without the dog's company, Nykola again felt frightened. The only light came from the stove. Shadows danced in the far corners of the room. But they were just shadows, he told himself. There was nothing there really. Why should he worry? He was warm and well fed. He had Sooty to warn him if an animal came into the clearing in the night. The sensible thing to do was to go to bed. He banked the fire, spread his blanket on the empty bunk and climbed in. In spite of his fears, he slept.

CHAPTER 15

Vigil at the Crossroads

Sooty woke him at dawn the next morning. The fire had gone out. Nykola lay shivering in his blanket for a few minutes before getting up.

"Hey, it's cold, Sooty, old boy!"

He opened the door and saw the ground was covered with a dusting of snow.

"Oh, no!" he groaned. "We're going to have a cold wait at the crossroads."

I wish I knew what time the priest is coming, he thought. I may have to wait most of the day. Or I might miss him, if I don't hurry.

Quickly, he cleaned out the stove and re-laid the fire. As far as he could see, everything looked the same as it had when he came in. When the Englishman returned, he would just have to set a match to the stove and he'd soon be warm.

Too bad there'd be no stove at the crossroads! If he took some matches, he could gather branches and twigs from the bush and light a fire to keep him warm while he waited.

He hesitated with his hand on the matchbox. Would the Englishman think he was a thief? Well, someday he would tell him what he had done and give him a whole boxful. Carefully, he counted out six matches. Opening the lard pail, he took out a slice of bread for himself and Sooty and put in the matches. Then he shouldered his blanket roll, pulled the door carefully shut, and started off.

Sooty had made tracks all around the shack, but beyond the clearing, the snow lay unbroken. No wild creatures had come near in the night. The path to the road seemed much shorter in the morning light, and soon the boy and the dog reached the edge of the woods. Sooty, who had been racing off into the bush and back, suddenly stopped and pricked up his ears.

Nykola halted.

"What is it, boy?" he asked uneasily.

He listened intently. From far away, he heard the creaking of a cart and men's voices. Who could it be? Not the priest! He

wouldn't use this road. Who would? Nykola bent down and grasped Sooty's fur. Soon, a wagon came in sight. Two oxen were pulling it. One was Bess. Behind the wagon walked Wasyl and their neighbour, Matey. Nykola almost shouted for joy. Then he remembered where he was going. His father would be angry. He would make Nykola go home with him and Granny would not see the priest. Why were the men going home? Nykola wondered. Was there no work for them? He couldn't tell from their expressions whether they were happy or sad. They just looked cold. As they came nearer, he drew back into the shadow of the trees.

But Sooty broke away and bounced out through the grass, barking joyously.

"What's this? The pup?" said Wasyl in amazement. "Where did you come from, you rascal!"

Both men stared around. Their breath hung in puffs in the cold air. They shouted.

"I wonder how he came here," said Wasyl.

"Must have wandered away from home," Matey said. "After a rabbit, maybe." He picked up the little dog.

"Well, pup, you've had a long walk! You'd better ride."

He put the puppy in the wagon, prodded the oxen, and they all moved off down the road toward home.

Nykola stepped out from the bush, opened his mouth to call, then closed it again. He wanted to go home instead of going to wait in the cold for the priest. Maybe he would miss the Father anyway. It would be a long walk home and he'd have to stay in the shack without Sooty for company. Again he almost shouted to his father. But in his imagination, he heard Granny beg him to go for the priest. He would go on. On the other hand, when Wasyl reached home and found him missing, he would be very angry. Even if Nykola brought the priest, Wasyl wouldn't let him into the house. What was the use of going on?

He ran out to the road, but he was too late. They were out of hearing around a bend. Should he run after them? He could easily catch up. But he hesitated. No, he must help Granny. He turned around and began to walk to the crossroads. There, the snow told him that the priest had not passed by that day. The only tracks were those made by his father and Matey coming from the north and turning onto their own road. No one had come from the south since the snow fell.

From the nearby bush Nykola gathered an armful of broken branches. The snow had not soaked the wood and he soon had a fire going. Even with the fire, it was too cold to stand around waiting. One thing he could do was stockpile wood, since he might have to feed the flames for several hours. Even though he didn't dare go too far into the bush in case the merchant's wagon should pass while he was out of sight, in an hour he had gathered more wood than he could burn that day. Still they had not come. What could he do next? It was so lonely! If only Sooty hadn't run out to his father, he would have the dog to play with.

He felt as if he were the only living thing around. The nearest people were at least a mile away. It was too late for birds. There might be rabbits in the woods, but he hadn't seen any. There was nothing to do but wait. Maybe he should start walking south. But, then, if he didn't meet them, he'd have a much longer walk back. He hoped he wouldn't have to spend another night in the Englishman's shack. Granny had said that the priest would come today. But Granny could have misunderstood the peddler. Or the peddler could have been wrong. Or the priest might have been delayed somewhere. He might have to go somewhere else first. Or he might not be coming at all!

This is silly, he thought. I'm just scaring myself!

He began to walk up and down the road, setting himself a course to follow: so many paces south, turn, come back and throw a stick on the fire; so many paces north, turn; and so on, back and forth. Although the sun was now shining brightly, the air was still cold and the snow had not melted. He made patterns in it as he paced, amusing himself by making a different pattern at each turn.

How quiet and still and lonely it was! He thought of his home. Father would likely be there now. All six of them would be crowded together in one room. It would be warm. But no one would be very comfortable if Wasyl was shouting angrily about his son going off for the priest! Or was Granny so sick—or even dead—that they were all perfectly quiet? Better not think about that. Think about something else. The ship. How crowded it had been on the ship. Then, he had longed to escape from people; now, he would be glad to see anyone.

A sound broke the stillness. Someone was coming. Nykola hurried to the fire and stood beside it, staring down the Dauphin road. His heart beat fast. Would this be the two men he was waiting for? At any moment he expected to see a plodding ox pulling a farm wagon.

It was a great shock, then, when a horse came into sight, hitched to what looked like a cabin on wheels. Nykola had never spoken to anyone who drove a horse. In the Ukraine, only rich landlords owned horses. In Canada, he had never even seen one since leaving Winnipeg. He stared in dismay. He wouldn't dare call to the driver to stop. Fortunately, he didn't have to. The odd-looking wagon drew up beside the fire. Two men looked out from a window over a slit through which the reins hung. One of them beckoned and Nykola walked slowly toward the wagon. The door opened and Martin Staranchuk leaned out.

"Who are you?" he asked. "What are you doing here?"

Nykola touched his cap.

"I came to meet the priest, Your Honour," he said.

"I'm here," called a voice from inside the cabin. "Step up, my son. It's too cold for you to stand there."

Martin frowned slightly, but he reached out and helped the boy climb into the wagon. Nykola was surprised at how young the priest looked. His hair and beard were golden, his face unlined. He was broad shouldered, but seemed slim beside the thick, stocky figure of the merchant.

"We must be getting on, Father," said Martin.

"Yes, yes, just let me hear what the boy has to say." The priest's voice was deep, but the tone gentle.

"Father, Your Honour," stammered Nykola, "Granny...Granny is sick. She wants to see you. She thinks she is dying, Father." The priest was looking at him kindly. Nykola felt bolder. "She wants to say her confession, Father. Will you come?"

"Come where?" growled the merchant. "Nobody lives near here. Who are you?"

"Nykola Ganczer, sir. My father is Wasyl Ganczer."

"I know him. He wouldn't give a cent for the church. Don't tell me he sent you for the priest!"

"No, sir." Nykola looked at the priest anxiously. "My Granny is Tetiana Doroshenko. She brought me here from the old country. And now she's very sick and wants to see a priest. So I've come to find you."

The Father smiled at Nykola.

"Couldn't we go to this old woman?" he asked Martin.

"Father, it would take us hours," protested the merchant. "We're expected in Wolf River tonight. Everyone will be waiting for us."

"Still," said the priest mildly, "your horse travels fast. It's a good animal. I think we must spare the time to see a dying woman who needs me."

Martin grunted with annoyance.

"People who helped to pay for your trip are waiting for you. Why should you waste time with Ganczer's family?"

Nykola remembered the coin Granny had given him. He held it out to the priest.

"Granny sent this to you, sir. It's for the church, she said. Or," his voice sank to a whisper, "to light candles for her soul, if she dies."

The priest took the coin.

"Thank you, my son." He spoke again

to his driver. “I think we must go to visit the sick. In our Lord’s name.”

“But I have goods on the wagon that I want to put into the store today! People will be in town for the weddings and christenings. They’ll buy the goods.”

“The weddings and christenings cannot take place without me.” The priest laughed gently. “The people will be there tomorrow, if we don’t arrive in time to perform the sacraments today. I will go to Tetiana Doroshenko.”

Nykola jumped down, kicked out the fire, grabbed his lard pail and was soon seated among the flour bags on the floor of the wagon. He had done it! He had met the priest and was taking him to Granny!

CHAPTER 16

Ukrainian Soil and Canadian Earth

At first, Nykola was shy with the two men. He could feel the merchant's resentment at having to go so far out of his way and he was very much in awe of the priest. Nevertheless, the ride was a great treat. The cabin was warm and his seat among the flour bags, comfortable. A window in the back wall gave him a view of the road they had passed. The horse was certainly swift. He compared the speed at which they moved now with his slow walk yesterday. Twisting to look out the front window, he saw the tracks that his father and Matey had made that morning. Even though they had been moving at the oxen's slow pace, the men would have been home long ago.

He wondered uneasily whether his father was angry. When he had started out to find the priest, he thought that his father would be away from home. The visit should have been over long before Wasyl heard of it.

The thought made Nykola uncomfortably warm. He pulled off his hat and laid it beside his mittens. Martin picked it up with one hand, keeping the reins in the other.

"Where did you get this?" he asked.

"Mother made it for me, sir," answered Nykola. "From the skins of the rabbits we eat."

"You get lots of rabbits, do you?"

"Yes, sir. My sisters and I snare them. We eat the meat and cure the skins and Mother sews hats and mittens for us. And a blanket for the baby. It's soft and warm for him."

The driver looked thoughtful. "Could she make more, do you think? Enough for me to sell?"

Before Nykola could answer, the wagon dipped into a deep hole. All three of them were tipped to the right.

"How much farther, boy?" Martin asked angrily.

"Just half a mile, sir. That was Matey Tymochko's place we passed. My father's is next."

His father! Nykola was very nervous.

Should he warn the priest that his father might be angry? Anyway, it was too late now. They were stopping in front of the house and his father was walking toward them.

Wasyl greeted the merchant politely and accepted the introduction to the priest quietly. But his eyes flashed with anger, and he did not bow as he would have done in the old country. This was a new land where the priests had no authority! Father Michael did not seem to expect him to bow. He greeted him with a friendly smile. To Nykola, Wasyl didn't speak at all. The boy's heart sank. His father *was* angry!

Father Michael said, "I had better see the old grandmother."

"I'll take you," said Nykola.

Marfa met them at the door. Larysa and Olaha were hiding behind the stove. Marfa curtsied low before the priest and poured out her thanks to him.

"I was glad to come, daughter. It's Martin Staranchuk you should thank," he said, with a twinkle in his eye. He peered around the room. "Where is Tetiana Doroshenko?"

The old woman struggled to a sitting position against the wall.

"Oh, Father, I am so glad to see you," she murmured.

He went to her and took her hand, patting it gently.

Turning to Marfa, he said, "Could I be alone to hear the confession, daughter?"

"Of course! Of course! Come, children!"

She coaxed the little girls out from behind the stove and handed them their outdoor clothing. While they dressed, Nykola whispered a question to his mother.

"Why is Father home?"

"The contractor had enough men. He didn't have any work for your father. Don't worry. It will be all right," she soothed as she saw his worried expression.

Leaving the baby asleep in his cradle, Marfa led the children outside.

"See if there's a rabbit in your snare," she said. "We'll need the meat."

There was a rabbit—the biggest the children had ever caught. As they hurried back to show it to their mother, they met her and Wasyl walking at the edge of the woods with the merchant.

"What a fine, big rabbit," said Martin. "That will make a beautiful skin."

Wasyl grinned at his children.

"Martin Staranchuk wants to buy all the rabbits you children can catch and skin," he said. "He's going to take the ones in the stable and leave us a bag of flour. So," he added, as he tweaked the tassel on Olaha's hat, "you little ones are beginning to earn your own way, eh?"

Nykola was amazed at the difference in his father's mood. A short time ago, he had looked so angry.

The change was explained when Martin, looking at the trees critically, said, "Yes, I can see you have a very good stand here. Some of the trees will make good lumber. You cut it and get your neighbour to help haul the logs to town. I'll have my sawmill set up by spring. As soon as the railway comes to Wolf River, the town will start to grow. Lumber will be needed for buildings. We'll make money, all of us."

Marfa's eyes sparkled. Here was a chance for Wasyl to get some cash and credit at the store. The coming of the priest seemed to have brought good luck.

Taking the rabbit from Nykola, she said, "I'll take him in and cook him. You and the good Father will eat before you go."

"No, no," protested Martin. "We must go as soon as we can. The folks in town expect us."

"Then you will take the rabbit," said Marfa. "A gift for the priest. From the children."

She glanced uneasily at her husband, but he made no objection.

"Thank you," said the merchant. "My wife will cook it for him tomorrow."

He placed the rabbit in the wagon and turned to find the priest standing in the doorway.

"Tetiana wishes to speak to you, Martin."

They all went indoors. Granny was lying down again. Her face was wet with tears. The merchant had to bend low to catch her words.

"Thank you, Martin Staranchuk, for bringing the blessed Father to me," she breathed.

"You must thank your grandson. He looked so cold and lonely there at the crossroads that we couldn't refuse him," he answered.

Nykola felt his cheeks flush as everyone smiled at him.

When the two men moved toward the door, Nykola went to sit on the floor beside Granny's bed. She took his hand.

"Now, if it is God's will to take me, I can die in peace, Nykolenko," she said.

Wasyl came in after seeing the visitors away. Nykola looked up at his father and rose slowly, letting the frail, old hand slip from his. The boy stood in silence. Wasyl stared at him. Twice he opened his mouth and closed it again. There was no sound in the room as his son waited for him to speak.

Finally, he said, "You disobeyed me, Nykola Ganczer."

"Yes, Father."

"Well, it has worked out for the best." Nykola relaxed at the mild tone. "I made a good deal with the merchant. We'll have credit at his store and perhaps cash as well." He stepped closer to the bed. "And you, old woman, are you happy now you've seen the priest?"

Granny smiled up at him.

"Very happy, Wasyl Ganczer, very happy. Now I feel at home in the new land." She turned and caught Nykola's eye. They smiled at one another.

* * * * *

Granny recovered and lived several more years during which the family moved into the large house that Wasyl built with boards from the new sawmill. She lived to care for three more of Marfa's babies, to help welcome Stefan Ganczer and his bride to the adjoining homestead, and to attend Larysa's wedding. Best of all, she lived to see her beloved Nykola file for a homestead.

To her great delight, Wasyl joined with the other settlers to purchase a plot of land for a church site and graveyard. This was located at the crossroads where Nykola had waited in the cold to meet the priest.

Here she was buried on August 30, 1908, exactly eight years after she and Nykola had run away together from Feodor Urbanovitch's farm in the Ukraine. After the men had lowered the coffin into the ground, Nykola and his mother stepped forward to the edge of the grave. Marfa held the wedding towel containing the earth that Granny had so lovingly scooped up before leaving her beloved homeland. Nykola opened the towel and reverently sprinkled the soil over the coffin.

"As you wished, Granny," he whispered. "Some of the Ukraine is buried with you."

ABOUT THE AUTHOR

Constance E. Horne was born and grew up in Winnipeg. She taught high school in Manitoba and British Columbia. She and her husband now live in Victoria where she does volunteer work with school children at the Art Gallery of Victoria. She has four grown-up children and two grandsons. This is her first published book.

Other books in the Jeanpac Series you might want to read:

The Ghost of Pirate Walk
by Jerry Williams

Day of the Wizards
by Jerry Williams

Dirt Bikes at Hangman's Clubhouse
by Sharon Siamon

Paddy Martel is Missing
by Beverley Spencer

The Ghost of Sullivan Town
by Beverley Spencer

The Treasure Hunt
by Sonia Craddock

The DNA Dimension
by Carol Matas

Mystery of the Ghostly Riders
by Lynn Manuel

Rebel Run
by D. Harold Turner